The Yellow Book of Richard Le Gallienne

Richard Thomas Gallienne was born in Liverpool on 20th January, 1866.

His first job was in an accountant's office, but this was quickly abandoned to pursue his first love as a professional writer. His first work, My Ladies' Sonnets, was published in 1887.

In 1889 he became, for a brief time, literary secretary to Wilson Barrett the manager, actor, and playwright. Barrett enjoyed immense success with the staging of melodramas, which would later reach a peak with the historical tragedy The Sign of the Cross (1895).

Le Gallienne joined the staff of The Star newspaper in 1891, and also wrote for various other papers under the pseudonym 'Logroller'. He contributed to the short-lived but influential quarterly periodical The Yellow Book, published between 1894 and 1897.

His first wife, Mildred Lee, died in 1894 leaving their daughter, Hesper, in his care.

In 1897 he married the Danish journalist Julie Norregard. However, the marriage would not be a success. She left him in 1903 and took their daughter Eva to live in Paris. They were eventually divorced in June 1911.

Le Gallienne now moved to the United States and became resident there.

On 27th October 1911, he married Mrs. Irma Perry, whose marriage to her first cousin, the painter and sculptor Roland Hinton Perry, had been dissolved in 1904. Le Gallienne and Irma had known each other for many years and had written an article together a few years earlier in 1906.

Le Gallienne and Irma lived in Paris from the late 1920s, where Irma's daughter Gwen was by then an established figure in the expatriate bohème. Le Gallienne also added a regular newspaper column to the frequent publication of his poems, essays and other articles.

By 1930 Le Gallienne's book publishing career had virtually ceased. During the latter years of that decade Le Gallienne lived in Menton on the French Riviera and, during the war years, in nearby Monaco. His house was commandeered by German troops and his handsome library was nearly sent back to Germany as bounty. Le Gallienne managed a successful appeal to a German officer in Monaco which allowed him to return to Menton to collect his books.

To his credit Le Gallienne refused to write propaganda for the local German and Italian authorities, and financially was often in dire need. On one occasion he collapsed in the street due to hunger.

Richard Thomas Gallienne died on 15th September 1947. He is buried in Menton in a grave whose lease is, at present, due to expire in 2023.

During the Victorian era the publishing of magazines and periodicals accelerated at a phenomenal rate. This really was mass market publishing to a hungry audience eager for literary sustenance. Many of our greatest authors contributed and expanded their reach whilst many fledging authors also found a ready source for their nascent works and careers.

Amongst the very many was 'The Yellow Book'. Although titled as 'An Illustrated Quarterly' it was sold as a cloth-bound hardback and within were short stories, essays, poetry, illustrations and portraits. It was edited by the American author Henry Harland, who also contributed, and its art editor was no less that the formidable Aubrey Beardsley, the enfant terrible of illustration.

Its yellow cover and name gave it an association with the risqué and erotic yellow covered works published in France. It was a visual shorthand for ideas that would push many boundaries of Society to more open interpretations. Being complete in each volume and slightly aloof it stayed away from serialised fiction and advertisements.

Within each lavishly illustrated edition were literary offerings that included works by such luminaries as Henry James, H G Wells, W B Yeats, Edith Nesbit, George Gissing and many others from the ascetic and decadent movements of the time.

The other notable inclusion was women both as contributors and amongst its editing staff, which was at odds with the then patriarchal gender norms.

Although it only survived for 13 issues its reach and influence were second to none.

Index of Contents

Tree-Worship

Vast and mysterious brother, 'ere was yet of me
   So much as men may poise upon a needle's end,
Still shook with laughter all this monstrous might of thee,
   And still with haughty crest it called the morning friend.

Thy latticed column jetted up the bright blue air,
   Tall as a mast it was, and stronger than a tower;
Three hundred winters had beheld thee mighty there,
   Before my little life had lived one little hour.

With rocky foot stern-set like iron in the land,
   With leafy rustling crest the morning sows with pearls,
Huge as a minster, half in heaven men saw thee stand,
   Thy rugged girth the waists of fifty Eastern girls.

Knotted and warted, slabbed and armoured like the hide
   Of tropic elephant; unstormable and steep
As some grim fortress with a princess-pearl inside,
   Where savage guardian faces beard the bastioned keep:

So hard a rind, old tree, shielding so soft a heart,
   A woman's heart of tender little nestling leaves;
Nor rind so hard but that a touch so soft can part,
   And spring s first baby-bud an easy passage cleaves.

I picture thee within with dainty satin sides,
   Where all the long day through the sleeping dryad dreams,
But when the moon bends low and taps thee thrice she glides,
   Knowing the fairy knock, to bask within her beams.

And all the long night through, for him with eyes and ears,
   She sways within thine arms and sings a fairy tune,
Till, startled with the dawn, she softly disappears,
   And sleeps and dreams again until the rising moon.

But with the peep of day great bands of heavenly birds
   Fill all thy branchy chambers with a thousand flutes,
And with the torrid noon stroll up the weary herds,
   To seek thy friendly shade and doze about thy roots;

Till with the setting sun they turn them once more home:
   And, ere the moon dawns, for a brief enchanted space,

Weary with million miles, the sore-spent star-beams come,
    And moths and bats hold witches sabbath in the place.

And then I picture thee some bloodstained Holyrood,
    Dread haunted palace of the bat and owl, whence steal,
Shrouded all day, lost murdered spirits of the wood,
    And fright young happy nests with homeless hoot and squeal.

Some Rizzio nightingale that plained adulterous love
Beneath the boudoir-bough of some fast-married bird,
Some dove that cooed to some one else s lawful dove,
And felt the dagger-beak pierce while his lady heard.

Then, maybe, dangling from thy gloomy gallows boughs,
A human corpse swings, mournful, rattling bones and chains—
His eighteenth century flesh hath fattened nineteenth century cows—
Ghastly AEolian harp fingered of winds and rains.

Poor Rizpah comes to reap each newly-fallen bone
That once thrilled soft, a little limb, within her womb;
And mark yon alchemist, with zodiac-spangled zone,
Wrenching the mandrake root that fattens in the gloom.

So rounds thy day, from maiden morn to haunted night,
From larks and sunlit dreams to owl and gibbering ghost;
A catacomb of dark, a sponge of living light,
To the wide sea of air a green and welcome coast.

I seek a god, old tree: accept my worship, thou!
All other gods have failed me always in my need.
I hang my votive song beneath thy temple bough,
Unto thy strength I cry—Old monster, be my creed!

Give me to clasp this earth with feeding roots like thine,
To mount yon heaven with such star-aspiring head,
Fill full with sap and buds this shrunken life of mine,
And from my boughs O might such stalwart sons be shed!

With loving cheek pressed close against thy horny breast,
I hear the roar of sap mounting within thy veins;
Tingling with buds, thy great hands open towards the west,
To catch the sweetheart wind that brings the sister rains.

O winds that blow from out the fruitful mouth of God,
O rains that softly fall from his all-loving eyes,
You that bring buds to trees and daisies to the sod,
O God s best Angel of the Spring, in me arise.

Home...

"We're going home!" I heard two lovers say,
   They kissed their friends and bade them bright good-byes;
   I hid the deadly hunger in my eyes,
And, lest I might have killed them, turned away.
Ah, love, we too once gambolled home as they,
   Home from the town with such fair merchandise,—
   Wine and great grapes—the happy lover buys:
A little cosy feast to crown the day.

Yes! we had once a heaven we called a home,
Its empty rooms still haunt me like thine eyes
   When the last sunset softly faded there;
Each day I tread each empty haunted room,
   And now and then a little baby cries,
   Or laughs a lovely laughter worse to bear.

Song

She's somewhere in the sunlight strong,
   Her tears are in the falling rain,
She calls me in the wind's soft song,
   And with the flowers she comes again;

Yon bird is but her messenger,
   The moon is but her silver car,
Yea! sun and moon are sent by her,
   And every wistful, waiting star.

Four Prose Fancies

I.—On Loving One's Enemies

Like all people who live apart from it, the Founder of the Christian religion was possessed of a profound knowledge of the world. As, according to the proverb, the woodlander sees nothing of the wood, because of its trees, so those who live in the world know nothing of it. They know its gaudy, glittering surface, its Crystal Palace fireworks, and the paste-diamonds with which it bedecks itself; they know its music halls and its night clubs, its Piccadillies and its politics, its restaurants and its salons; but of the bad—or good?—heart of it all, they know nothing. In more meanings than one, it takes a saint to catch a sinner; and Christ certainly knew as well as saved the sinner.

But none of His precepts show a truer knowledge of life and its conditions than His commandment that we should love our enemies. He realised—can we doubt?—that without enemies the Church He bade His followers build could not hope to be established. He knew that the spiritual fire He strove to kindle would spread but a little unless the four winds of the world blew against it. Well, indeed, may the Christian Church love its enemies, for it is they who have made it.

Indeed, for a man, or a cause, that wants to get on there is nothing like a few hearty, zealous enemies. Most of us would never be heard of if it were not for our enemies. The unsuccessful man counts up his friends, but the successful man numbers his enemies. A friend of mine was lamenting, the other day, that he could not find twelve people to disbelieve in him. He had been seeking them for years, he sighed, and could not get beyond eleven. But, even so, with only eleven he was a very successful man. In these kind-hearted days enemies are becoming so rare that one has to go out of one's way to make them. The true interpretation, therefore, of the easiest of the commandments is—make your enemies, and your enemies will make you.

So soon as the armed men begin to spring up in our fields, we may be sure we have not sown in vain.

Properly understood, an enemy is but a negative embodiment of our personalities or ideas. He is the involuntary witness to our vitality. Much as he despises us, greatly as he may injure us, he is none the less a creature of our making. It was we who put into him the breath of his malignity, and inspired the activity of his malice. Therefore, with his very existence so tremendous a tribute, we can afford to smile at his self-conscious disclaimers of our significance. Though he slay us, we made him—to "make an enemy," is not that the phrase?

Indeed, the fact that he is our enemy is his one raison d'être. That alone should make us charitable to him. Live and let live. Without us our enemy has no occupation, for to hate us is his profession. Think of his wives and families!

The friendship of the little for the great is an old-established profession; there is but one older—namely, the hatred of the little for the great; and, though it is perhaps less officially recognised, it is without doubt the more lucrative. It is one of the shortest roads to fame. Why is the name of Pontius Pilate an uneasy ghost or history? Think what fame it would have meant to be an enemy of Socrates or Shakespeare! Blackwood's Magazine and The Quarterly Review only survive to-day because they once did their best to strangle the genius of Keats and Tennyson. Two or three journals of our own time, by the same unfailing method, seek that circulation from posterity which is denied them in the present.

This is particularly true in literature, where the literary enemy is as organised a tradesman as the literary agent. Like the literary agent, he naturally does his best to secure the biggest men. No doubt the time will come when the literary cut-throat—shall we call him?—will publish dainty little books of testimonials from authors, full of effusive gratitude for the manner in which they have been slashed and bludgeoned into fame. "Butcher to Mr. Grant Allen" may then become a familiar legend over literary shop-fronts:

Ah! did you stab at Shelley's heart
With silly sneer and cruel lie?
And Wordsworth, Tennyson, and Keats,
To murder did you nobly try?

You failed, 'tis true; but what of that?
The world remembers still your name—
'Tis fame, for you, to be the cur
That barks behind the heels of Fame.

Any one who is fortunate enough to have enemies will know that all this is far from being fanciful. If one's enemies have any other raison d'être beyond the fact of their being our enemies—what is it? They are neither beautiful nor clever, wise nor good, famous, nor, indeed, passably distinguished. Were they any of these, they would not have taken to so humble a means of getting their living. Instead of being our enemies, they could then have afforded to employ enemies on their own account.

Who, indeed, are our enemies? Broadly speaking, they are all those people who lack what we possess.

If you are rich, every poor man is necessarily your enemy. If you are beautiful, the great democracy of the plain and ugly will mock you in the streets.

It will be the same with everything you possess. The brainless will never forgive you for possessing brains, the weak will hate you for your strength, and the evil for your good heart. If you can write, all the bad writers are at once your foes. If you can paint, the bad painters will talk you down. But more than any talent or charm you may possess, the pearl of price for which you will be most bitterly hated will be your success. You can be the most wonderful person that ever existed so long as you don't succeed, and nobody will mind. "It is the sunshine," says someone, "that brings out the adder." So powerful, indeed, is success that it has been known to turn a friend into a foe. Those, then, who wish to engage a few trusty enemies out of place need only advertise among the unsuccessful.

P.S.—For one service we should be particularly thankful to our enemies they save us so much in stimulants. Their unbelief so helps our belief, their negatives make us so positive.

II.—The Dramatic Art of Life

It is a curious truth that, whereas in every other art deliberate choice of method and careful calculation of effect are expected from the artist, in the greatest and most difficult art of all, the art of life, this is not so. In literature, painting, or sculpture you first evolve your conception, and then after long study of it, as it still glows and shimmers in your imagination, you set about the reverent selection of that form which shall be its most truthful incarnation, in words, in paint, in marble. Now life, as has been said many times, is an art too. Sententious morality from time past has told us that we are each given a part to play, evidently implying, with involuntary cynicism, that the art of life is—the art of acting!

As with the actor we are each given a certain dramatic conception for the expression of which we have precisely the same artistic materials—namely, our own bodies, sometimes including heart and brains. One has often heard the complaint of a certain actor that he acts himself. On the metaphorical stage of life the complaint and the implied demand are just the reverse. How much more interesting life would be if only more people had the courage and skill to act themselves, instead of abjectly understudying some one else. Of course, there are supers on the stage of life as on the real stage. It is proper that these should dress and speak and think alike. These one courteously excepts from the generalisation that the composer of the play, as Marcus Aurelius calls him, has given us a certain part to play—that part simply oneself: a part, need one say, by no means as easy as it seems; a part most difficult to study, and requiring daily rehearsal. So difficult is it, indeed, that most people throw up the part, and join the ranks of the supers—who, curiously enough, are paid much more handsomely than the principals. They enter one of the learned or idle professions, join the army or take to trade, and so speedily rid themselves of the irksome necessity of being anything more individual than "the learned counsel," "the learned judge," "my lord bishop," or "the colonel," names impersonal in application as the dignity of "Pharaoh," whereof the name and not the man was alone important. Henceforth they are the Church, the Law, the Army, the City, or that vaguer profession, Society. Entering one of these, they become as lost to the really living world as the monk who voluntarily surrenders all will and character of his own at the threshold of his monastery: bricks in a prison wall, privates in the line, peas in a row. But, as I say, these are the parts that pay. For playing the others, indeed, you are not paid, but expected to pay—dearly.

It is full time we turned to those on whom falls the burden of those real parts. Such, when quite young, if they be conscientious artists, will carefully consider themselves, their gifts and possibilities, study to discover their artistic raison d'être and how best to fulfil it. He or she will say: Here am I, a creature of great gifts and exquisite sensibilities, drawn by great dreams, and vibrating to great emotions; yet this potent and exquisite self is as yet, I know, but unwrought material of the perfect work of art it is intended that I should make of it—but the marble where upon with patient chisel I must liberate the perfect and triumphant ME! As a poet listening with trembling ear to the voice of his inspiration, so I tremulously ask myself—what is the divine conception that is to become embodied in me, what is the divine meaning of ME? How best shall I express it in look, in word, in deed, till my outer self becomes the truthful symbol of my inner self—till, in fact, I have successfully placed the best of myself on the outside!—for others besides myself to see, and know and love!

What is my part, and how am I to play it?

Returning to the latter image, there are two difficulties that beset one in playing a part on the stage of life, right at the outset. You are not allowed to "look" it, or "dress" it! What would an actor think, who, asked to play Hamlet, found that he would be expected to play it without make-up and in nineteenth-century costume? Yet many of us are in a like dilemma with similar parts. Actors and audience must all wear the same drab clothes and the same immobile expression. It is in vain you protest that you do not really belong to this absurd and vulgar nineteenth century, that you have been spirited into it by a cruel mistake, that you really belong to mediaeval Florence, to Elizabethan, Caroline, or at latest Queen Anne England, and that you would like to be allowed to look and dress as like it as possible. It is no use; if you dare to look or dress like anything but your own tradesmen—and other critics—it is at your peril. If you are beautiful, you are expected to disguise a fact that is an open insult to every other person you look at; and you must, as a general rule, never look, wear, feel, or say what everybody else is not also looking, wearing, feeling, or saying.

Thus you get some hint of the difficulty of playing the part of yourself on this stage of life. In these matters of dressing and looking your part musicians seem granted an immunity denied to all their fellow-artists. Perhaps it is taken for granted that the musician is a fool—the British public is so intuitive. Yet it takes the same view of the poet—without allowing him a like immunity. And, by the way, what a fine conception of his part had Tennyson: of the dignity, the mystery, the picturesqueness of it. Tennyson would have felt it an artistic crime to look like his publisher; yet what poet is there left us to-day half so distinguished-looking as his publisher?

Indeed, curiously enough, among no set of men does the desire to look as commonplace as the rest of the world seem so strong as among men of letters. Perhaps it is out of consideration for the rest of the world; but whatever the reason, immobility of expression and general mediocrity of style are more characteristic of them at present than even the military.

It is surely a strange paradox that we should pride ourselves on schooling to foolish insensibility, on eliminating from them every mark of individual character, the faces that were intended subtly and eloquently to image our moods—to look glad when we are glad, sorry when we are sorry, angry in anger, and lovely in love.

The impassivity of the modern young man is indeed a weird and wonderful thing. Is it a mark to hide from us the appalling sins he none the less openly affects? Is it meant to conceal that once in his life he paid a wild visit to "The Empire"—by kind indulgence of the County Council? that he once chucked a barmaid under the chin, that he once nearly got drunk, that he once spoke to a young lady he did not know—and then ran away?

One sighs for the young men of the days of Gautier and Hugo, the young men with red waistcoats who made asses of themselves at first nights and on the barricades, young men with romance in their hearts and passion in their blood, fearlessly sentimental and picturesquely everything.

The lover then was not ashamed that you should catch radiant glimpses of his love in his eyes—nay! if you smiled kindly on him, he would take you by the arm and insist on your breaking a bottle with him in honour of his mistress. Joy and sorrow then wore their appropriate colours, according, so to say, to the natural sumptuary laws of the emotions—one of which is that the right place for the heart is the sleeve.

It is the duty of those who are great, or to whom great destinies of joy or sorrow have been dealt, to wear their distinctions for the world to see. It is good for the world, which in its crude way indicates the rudiments of this dramatic art of life, when it decrees that the bride shall walk radiant in orange blossom, and the mourner sadden our streets with blacks—symbols ever passing before us of the moving vicissitudes of life.

The mourner cannot always be sad, or the bride merry; the bride indeed sometimes weeps at the altar, and the mourner laughs a savage cynical laugh at the grave; but for those moments in which they awhile forget parts more important than themselves, the tailor and the dressmaker have provided symbolical garments, just as military decorations have been provided for heroes without the gift of looking heroic, and sacerdotal vestments for the priest, who, like a policeman, is not always on duty.

In playing his part the conscientious artist in life, like any other actor, must often seem to feel more than he really feels at a given moment, say more than he means. In this he is far from being insincere— though he must make up his mind to be accused daily of insincerity and affectation. On the contrary, it will be his very sincerity that necessitates his make-believe. With his great part ever before him in its inspiring completeness, he must be careful to allow no merely personal accident of momentary feeling or action to jeopardise the general effect. There are moments, for example, when a really true lover, owing to such masterful natural facts as indigestion, a cold, or extreme sleepiness, is unable to feel all that he knows he really feels. To "tell the truth," as it is called under such circumstances, would simply be a most dangerous form of lying. There is no duty we owe to truth more imperative than that of lying stoutly on occasion—for, indeed, there is often no other way of conveying the whole truth than by telling the part-lie.

A watchful sincerity to our great conception of ourselves is the first and last condition of our creating that finest work of art—a personality; for a personality, like a poet, is not only born, but made.

III.—The Arbitrary Classification of Sex

In an essay on Vauvenargues Mr. John Morley speaks with characteristic causticity of those epigrammatists "who persist in thinking of man and woman as two different species," and who make verbal capital out of the fancied distinction in the form of smart epigrams beginning "Les femmes." It is one of Shakespeare's cardinal characteristics that he understood woman. Mr. Meredith's fame as a novelist is largely due to the fact that he too understands women. The one spot on the sun of Robert Louis Stevenson's fame, so we are told, is that he could never draw a woman. His capacity for drawing men counted for nothing, apparently, beside this failure. Evidently the Sphinx has not the face of a woman for nothing. That is why no one has yet read her riddle, translated her mystic smile. Yet many people smile mysteriously, without any profound meanings behind their smile, with no other reason than a desire to mystify. Perhaps the Sphinx smiles to herself just for the fun of seeing us take her smile so seriously. And surely women must so smile as they hear their psychology so gravely discussed. Of course, the superstition is invaluable to them, and it is only natural that they should make the most of it. Man is supposed to be a complete ignoramus in regard to all the specialised female "departments"—from the supreme mystery of the female heart to the humble domestic mysteries of a household. Similarly, men are supposed to have no taste in women's dress, yet for whom do women clothe themselves in the rainbow and the sea-foam, if not to please men? And was not the high-priest of that delicious and fascinating mystery a man—if it be proper to call the late M. Worth a man?—as the best cooks are men, and the best waiters?

It would seem to be assumed from all this mystification that men are beings clear as daylight, both to themselves and to women. Poor simple manageable souls, their wants are easily satisfied, their psychology—which, it is implied, differs little from their physiology—long since mapped out.

It may be so, but it is the opinion of some that men's simplicity is no less a fiction than women's mysterious complexity, and that human character is made up of much the same qualities in men and women, irrespective of a merely rudimentary sexual distinction, which has, of course, its proper importance, and which the present writer would be the last to wish away. From that quaint distinction of sex springs, of course, all that makes life in the smallest degree worth living, from great religions to tiny flowers. Love and beauty and poetry; "Romeo and Juliet," "Helen of Troy," Shakespeare's plays, Burne-Jones's pictures, and Wagner's operas—all such moving expressions of human life, as a great scientist has shown us, spring from the all-important fact that "male and female created He them."

This everybody knows, and few are fool enough to deny. Many people, however, confuse this organic distinction of sex with its time-worn conventional symbols; just as religion is commonly confused with its external rites and ceremonies. The comparison naturally continues itself further; for, as in religion so soon as some traditional garment of the faith has become outworn or otherwise unsuitable, and the proposal is made to dispense with or substitute it, an outcry immediately is raised that religion itself is in danger—so with sex, no sooner does one or the other sex propose to discard its arbitrary conventional characteristics, or to supplement them by others borrowed from its fellow-sex, than an outcry immediately is raised that sex itself is in danger.

Sex—the most potent force in the universe—in danger because women wear knickerbockers instead of petticoats, or military men take to corsets and cosmetics!

That parallel with religion may be pursued profitably one step further. In religion, the test of your faith is not how you live, not in your kindness of heart or purity of mind, but how you believe—in the Trinity, in the Atonement; and do you turn to the East during the recital of the Apostles' Creed? These and such, as everyone knows, are the vital matters of religion. And it is even so with sex. You are not asked for the realities of manliness or womanliness; but for the shadows, the arbitrary externalities, the fashion of which changes from generation to generation.

To be truly womanly you must never wear your hair short; to be truly manly you must never wear it long. To be truly womanly you must dress as daintily as possible, however uncomfortably; to be truly manly you must wear the most hideous gear ever invented by the servility of tailors—a strange succession of cylinders from head to heel; cylinder on head, cylinder round your body, cylinders on arms and cylinders on legs. To be truly womanly you must be shrinking and clinging in manner and trivial in conversation, you must have no ideas and rejoice that you wish for none; you must thank Heaven that you have never ridden a bicycle or smoked a cigarette; and you must be prepared to do a thousand other absurd and ridiculous things. To be truly manly you must be and do the opposite of all these things, with this exception—that with you the possession of ideas is optional. The finest specimens of British manhood are without them, but that, I say, is, generally speaking, a matter for yourself. It is indeed the only matter in which you have any choice. More important matters, such as the cut of your clothes and hair, the shape of your face, the length of your moustache and the pattern of your cane—all these are very properly regulated for you by laws of fashion, which you could never dream of breaking. You may break every moral law there is—or rather, was—and still remain a man. You may be a bully, a cad, a coward and a fool in the poor heart and brains of you; but so long as you wear the mock regimentals of contemporary manhood, and are above all things plain and undistinguished enough, your reputation for manhood will be secure. There is nothing so dangerous to a reputation for manhood as brains or beauty.

In short, to be a true woman you have only to be pretty and an idiot, and to be a true man you have only to be brutal and a fool.

From these misconceptions of manliness and womanliness, these superstitions of sex, many curious confusions have come about. The, so to say, professional differentiation between the sexes had at one time gone so far that men were credited with the entire monopoly of a certain set of human qualities, and women with the monopoly of a certain set of other human qualities; yet every one of these are qualities which one would have thought were proper to, and necessary for, all human beings alike, male and female.

In a dictionary of a date (1856) when everything on earth and in heaven was settled and written in penny cyclopedias and books of deportment, I find these delicious definitions:

Manly: becoming a man; firm; brave; undaunted; dignified; noble; stately; not boyish or womanish.

Womanly: becoming a woman; feminine; as womanly behaviour.

Under Woman we find the adjectives—soft, mild, pitiful and flexible, kind, civil, obliging, humane, tender, timorous, modest.

Who can doubt that the dictionary maker defined and distributed his adjectives aright for the year 1856? Since then, however, many alarming heresies have taken root steadily in our land, and some are heard to declare that both these sets of adjectives apply to men and women alike, and are, in facr, necessities of any decent human outfit. Otherwise the conclusion is obvious, that no one desirous of the adjective "manly" must ever be—soft, mild, pitiful and flexible, kind, civil, obliging, humane, tender, timorous, or modest; and no one desirous of the adjective "womanly"—be firm, brave, undaunted, dignified, noble, or stately.

But surely the essentials of "manliness" and "womanliness" belong to man and woman alike—the externals are purely artistic considerations, and subject to the vagaries of fashion. In art no one would think of allowing fashion any serious artistic opinion. It is usually the art which is out of fashion that is most truly art. Similarly, fashions in manliness or womanliness have nothing to do with real manliness or womanliness. Moreover, the adjectives "manly" or "womanly," applied to works of art, or the artistic surfaces of men and women, are irrelevant—that is to say, impertinent. You have no right to ask a poem or a picture to look manly or womanly, any more than you have any right to ask a man or a woman to look manly or womanly. There is no such thing as looking manly or womanly. There is looking beautiful or ugly, distinguished or commonplace. The one law or externals is beauty in all its various manifestations. To ask the sex of a beautiful person is as absurd as it would be to ask the publisher the sex of a beautiful book. Such questions are for midwives and doctors.

It was once the fashion for heroes to shed tears on the smallest occasion, and it does not appear that they fought the worse for it: some of the firmest, bravest, most undaunted, some dignified, most noble, most stately human beings have been women; as some of the softest, mildest, most pitiful and flexible, most kind, civil, obliging, humane, tender, timorous and modest human beings have been men. Indeed, the bravest men that ever trod this planet have worn corsets, and it needs more courage nowadays for a man to wear his hair long than to machine-gun a whole African nation. Moreover, quite the nicest women one knows ride bicycles—in the rational costume.

IV.—The Fallacy of a Nation

It is, I am given to understand, a familiar axiom of mathematics that no number of ciphers placed in front of significant units, or tens or hundreds of units, adds in the smallest degree to the numerical value of those units. The figure one becomes of no more importance however many noughts are marshalled in front of it—though, indeed, in the mathematics of human nature this is not so. Is not a man or woman considered great in proportion to the number of ciphers that walk in front of him, from a humble brace of domestics to guards of honour and imperial armies?

A parallel profound truth of mathematics is that a nought, however many times it be multiplied, remains nought; but again we find the reverse obtain in the mathematics of human nature. One might have supposed that the result of one nobody multiplied even fifty million times would still be nobody. However, such is far from being the case. Fifty million nobodies make—a nation. Of course, there is no need for so many. I am reckoning as a British subject, and speak of fifty million merely as an illustration of the general fact that it is the multiplication of nobodies that makes a nation. "Increase and multiply" was, it will be remembered, the recipe for the Jewish nation.

Nobodies of the same colour, tongues, and prejudices, have but to congregate together in a crowd sufficiently big for other similar crowds to recognise them, and they are given a name of their own, and become recognised as a nation—one of "the Great Powers."

Beyond those differences in colour, tongue, and prejudices, there is really no difference between the component units—or rather ciphers—of all these several national crowds. You have seen a procession of various trades-unions filing towards Hyde Park, each section with its particular banner of a strange device: "the United Guild of Paperhangers," "the Ancient Order of Plumbers," and so on. And you may have marvelled to notice how alike the members of the various carefully differentiated companies were. So to say, they each and all might have been plumbers; and you couldn't help feeling that it wouldn't have mattered much if some of the paperhangers had by mistake got walking amongst the plumbers, or vice versa.

So the great trades-unions of the world file past, one with the odd word "Russia" on its banner; another boasting itself "Germany"—this with a particularly bumptious and self-important young man walking backward in front of it, in the manner of a Salvation Army captain, and imperially waving an iron wand; still another "nation" calling itself "France"; and yet another boasting the biggest brass band, and called "England." Other smaller bodies of nobodies—that is, smaller nations—file past with a humbler tread— though there is really no need for their doing so. For, as we have said, they are in every particular like to those haughtier nations who take precedence of them. In fact, one or two of them such as Norway and Denmark—were a truer system of human mathematics to obtain—are really of more importance than the so-called greater nations, in that among their nobodies they include a larger percentage of intellectual somebodies.

Remembering that percentage of wise men, the formula of a nation were perhaps more truly stated in our first mathematical image. The wise men in a nation are as the units with the noughts in front of them. And when I say wise men I do not, indeed, mean merely the literary men or the artists, but all those somebodies with some real force of character, people with brains and hearts, fighters and lovers, saints and thinkers, and the patient industrious workers. Such, if you consider, are really no integral part of the nation among which they are cast. They have no part in what are grandiloquently called national interests—war, politics, and horse-racing to wit. A change of Government leaves them as unmoved as an election for the Board of Guardians. They would as soon think of entering Parliament or the County Council, as of yearning to manage the gasworks, or to go about with one of those carts bearing the legend "Aldermen and Burgesses of the City of London" conspicuously upon its front. Their main concern in political change is the rise and fall of the income-tax, and, be the Cabinet Tory or Liberal, their rate papers come in for the same amount. It is likely that national changes would affect them but little more. What would a foreign invasion mean more than that we should pay our taxes to French, Russian, or German officials, instead of to English ones? French and Italians do our cooking, Germans manage our music, Jews control our money markets; surely it would make little difference to us for France, Russia, or Germany to undertake our government. Japan, indeed, already dictates our foreign policy. The worst of being conquered by Russia would be the necessity of learning Russian; whereas a little rubbing up of our French would make us comfortable with France. Besides, to be conquered by France would save us crossing the Channel to Paris, and then we might hope for cafés in Regent Street, and an emancipated literature. As a matter of fact, so-called national interests are merely certain private interests on a large scale, the private interests of financiers, ambitious politicians and soldiers, and great merchants. Broadly speaking, there are no rival nations—there are rival markets, and it is its Board of Trade and its Stock Exchange rather than its Houses of Parliament that virtually govern a country. Thus one seaport goes down and another comes up, industries forsake one country to bless another, the military and naval strengths of nations fluctuate this way and that; and to those whom these changes affect they are undoubtedly important matters—the great capitalist, the soldier, and the politician; but to the quiet man at home with his wife, his children, his books and his flowers, to the artist busied with braver translunary matters, to the saint with his eyes filled with "the white radiance of eternity," to the shepherd on the hillside, the milkmaid in love, or the angler at his sport—what are these pompous commotions, these busy, bustling mimicries of reality? England will be just as good to live in though men some day call her France. Let the big busybodies divide her amongst them as they like, so that they leave one alone with one's fair share of the sky and the grass, and an occasional not too vociferous nightingale.

The reader will perhaps forgive the hackneyed reference to Sir Thomas Browne peacefully writing his Religio Medici amid all the commotions of the Civil War, and to Gautier calmly correcting the proofs of his new poems during the siege of Paris. The milkman goes his rounds amid the crash of empires. It is not his business to fight. His business is to distribute his milk—as much after half-past seven as may be inconvenient. Similarly, the business of the thinker is with his thought, the poet with his poetry. It is the business of politicians to make national quarrels, and the business of the soldier to fight them. But as for the poet—let him correct his proofs, or beware the printer.

The idea, then, of a nation is a grandiloquent fallacy in the interests of commerce and ambition— political and military. All the great and good, clever and charming people belong to one secret nation, for which there is no name unless it be the Chosen People. They are the lost tribes of love, art and religion, lost and swamped amid alien peoples, but ever dreaming of a time when they shall meet once more in Jerusalem.

Yet though they are thus aliens, taking and wishing no part in the organisation of the "nations" among which they dwell, this does not prevent those nations taking part and credit in them. And whenever a brave soldier wins a battle, or an intrepid traveller discovers a new land, his particular nation flatters itself as though it—the million nobodies—had done it. With a profound indifference to, indeed an active dislike of, art and poetry, there is nothing on which a nation prides itself so much as upon its artists and poets, whom, invariably, they starve, neglect, and even insult as long as it is not too silly to do so.

Thus the average Englishman talks of Shakespeare—as though he himself had written the plays; of India as though he himself had conquered it. And thus grow up such fictions as "national greatness" and "public opinion."

For what is "national greatness" but the glory reflected from the memories of a few great individuals? and what is "public opinion" but the blustering echoes of the opinion of a few clever young men on the morning papers?

For how can people in themselves little become great by merely congregating into a crowd, however large? And surely fools do not become wise, or worth listening to, merely by the fact of their banding together.

A "public opinion" on any matter except football, prize-fighting, and perhaps cricket, is merely ridiculous—by whatever brutal physical powers it may be enforced—ridiculous as a town council's opinion upon art; and a nation is merely a big fool with an army.

A Seventh-story Heaven

"Dans un grenier qu'on est bien à vingt ans!"

At one end of the city that I love there is a tall dingy pile of offices that has evidently seen more prosperous fortunes. It is not the aristocratic end. It is remote from the lordly street of the fine shops of the fair women, where in the summer afternoons the gay bank clerks parade arm-in-arm in the wake of the tempestuous petticoat. It lies aside from the great exchange which looks like a scene from Romeo and Juliet in the moonlight, from the town-hall from whose clocked and gilded cupola ring sweet chimes at midnight, and whence, throned above the city, a golden Britannia, in the sight of all men, is seen visibly ruling the waves; while in the square below the death of Nelson is played all day in stone, with a frieze of his noble words about the pedestal—England expects! What an influence that stirring challenge has yet upon the hearts of men may be seen by anyone who will study the faces of the busy, imaginative cotton-brokers, who, in the thronged and humming mornings, sell what they have never seen to a customer they will never see.

In fact, the end I mean is just the very opposite end to that. It is the end where the cotton that everybody sells and nobody buys is seen, piled in great white stacks, or swinging in the air from the necks of mighty cranes, that could nip up an elephant with as little ado, and set him down on the wharf, with a box on his ugly ears for his cowardly trumpeting. It is the end that smells of tar, the domain of the harbour-masters, where the sailor finds a "home,"—not too sweet, and where the wild sea is tamed in a maze of granite squares and basins; the end where the riggings and buildings rise side by side, and a clerk might swing himself out upon the yards from his top-floor desk. Here is the Custom House, and the conversation that shines is full of freightage and dock dues; here are the shops that sell nothing but oilskins, sextants and parrots, and here the taverns do a mighty trade in rum. It was in this quarter for a brief sweet time that Love and Beauty made their strange home, as though a pair of halcyons should choose to nest in the masthead of a cattleship. Love and Beauty chose this quarter, as alas, Love and Beauty must choose so many things—for its cheapness. Love and Beauty were poor, and office rents in this quarter were exceptionally low. But what should Love and Beauty do with an office? Love was a poor poet in need of a room for his bed and his rhymes, and Beauty was a little blue-eyed girl who loved him.

It was a shabby forbidding place, gloomy and comfortless as a warehouse on the banks of Styx. No one but Love and Beauty would have dared to choose it for their home. But Love and Beauty have a great confidence in themselves—a confidence curiously supported by history—and they never had a moment's doubt that this place was as good as another for an earthly Paradise. So Love signed an agreement for one great room at the very top, the very masthead of the building, and Beauty made it pretty with muslin curtains, flowers, and dainty makeshifts of furniture, but chiefly with the light of her own heavenly face. A stroke of luck coming one day to the poet, the lovers, with that extravagance which the poor alone have the courage to enjoy, procured a piano on the kind-hearted hire-purchase system, a system specially conceived for lovers. Then, indeed, for many a wonderful night that room was not only on the seventh floor, but in the seventh heaven; and as Beauty would sit at the piano, with her long hair flying loose, and her soul like a whirl of starlight about her brows, a stranger peering in across the soft lamplight, seeing her face, hearing her voice, would deem that the long climb, flight after flight of dreary stair, had been appropriately rewarded by a glimpse of Heaven.

Certainly it must have seemed a strange contrast from the life about and below it. The foot of that infernal stair plunged in the warm rum-and-thick-twist atmosphere of a sailors tavern—and "The Jolly Shipmates" was a house of entertainment by no means to be despised. Often have I sat there with the poet, drinking the whisky from which Scotland takes its name, among wondering sea-boots and sou'-westers, who could make nothing of that wild hair and that still wilder talk.

From the kingdom of rum and tar, you mounted into a zone of commission agents and ship-brokers, a chill unoccupied region, in which every small office-door bore the names of half-a-dozen different firms, and yet somehow could not contrive to look busy. Finally came an airy echoing landing, a region of empty rooms, which the landlords in vain recommended as studios to a city that loved not art. Here dwelt the keeper and his kind-hearted little wife, and no one besides save Love and Beauty. There was thus a feeling of rarefaction in the atmosphere, as though at this height it was only the Alpine flora of humanity that could find root and breathing. But once along the bare passage and through a certain door, and what a sudden translation it was into a gracious world of books and flowers and the peace they always bring.

Once upon a time, in that enchanted past where dwell all the dreams we love best, precisely—with loving punctuality—at five in the afternoon, a pretty girlish figure, like Persephone escaping from the shades, stole through the rough sailors at the foot of that sordid Jacob's ladder and made her way to the little Heaven at the top.

I shall not describe her, for the good reason that I cannot. Leonardo, ever curious of the beauty that was most strangely exquisite, once in an inspired hour painted such a face, a face wrought of the porcelain of earth with the art of Heaven. But, whoever should paint it, God certainly made it—must have been the comment of any one who caught a glimpse of that little figure vanishing heavenwards up that stair, like an Ascension of Fra Angelico's—that is any one interested in art and angels.

She had not long to wait outside the door she sought, for the poet, who had listened all day for the sound, had ears for the whisper of her skirts as she came down the corridor, and before she had time to knock had already folded her in his arms. The two babes in that thieves' wood of commission agents and ship-brokers stood silent together for a moment, in the deep security of a kiss such as the richest millionaire could never buy—and then they fell to comparing notes of their day's work. The poet had had one of his rare good days. He had made no money, his post had been even more disappointing than usual,—but he had written a poem, the best he had ever written, he said, as he always said of his last new thing. He had been burning to read it to somebody all afternoon—had with difficulty refrained from reading it to the loquacious little keeper's wife as she brought him some coals—so it was not to be expected that he should wait a minute before reading it to her whom indeed it strove to celebrate. With arms round each other's necks, they bent over the table littered with the new-born poem, all blots and dashes like the first draft of a composer's score, and the poet, deftly picking his way among the erasures and interlineations, read aloud the beautiful words—with a full sense of their beauty!—to ears that deemed them more beautiful even than they were. The owners of this now valuable copyright allow me to irradiate my prose with three of the verses.

"Ah! what," half-chanted, half-crooned the poet—

"Ah! what a garden is your hair!—
Such treasure as the kings of old,
In coffers of the beaten gold,
Laid up on earth—and left it there."

So tender a reference to hair whose beauty others beside the poet had loved must needs make a tender interruption—the only kind of interruption the poet could have forgiven and—" Who," he continued—

"Who was the artist of your mouth?
What master out of old Japan
Wrought it so dangerous to man . . . ."

And here it was but natural that laughter and kisses should once more interrupt—

"Those strange blue jewels of your eyes,
Painting the lily of your face,
What goldsmith set them in their place—
Forget-me-nots of Paradise.

"And that blest river of your voice,
Whose merry silver stirs the rest
Of waterlilies in your breast . . . ."

At last, in spite of more interruptions, the poem came to an end—whereupon, of course, the poet immediately read it through once more from the beginning, its personal and emotional elements, he felt, having been done more justice on a first reading than its artistic excellencies.

"Why, darling, it is splendid," was his little sweetheart's comment; "you know how happy it makes me to think it was written for me, don't you?" And she took his hands and looked up at him with eyes like the morning sky.

Romance in poetry is almost exclusively associated with very refined ethereal matters, stars and flowers and such like—happily, in actual life it is often associated with much humbler objects. Lovers, like children, can make their paradises out of the quaintest materials. Indeed, our paradises, if we only knew, are always cheap enough; it is our hells that are so expensive. Now these lovers—like, if I mistake not, many other true lovers before and since—when they were particularly happy, when some special piece of good luck had befallen them, could think of no better paradise than a little dinner together in their seventh-story heaven. "Ah! wilderness were Paradise enow!"

To-night was obviously such an occasion. But, alas! where was the money to come from? They didn't need much—for it is wonderful how happy you can be on five shillings if you only know how. At the same time it is difficult to be happy on nine-pence—which was the entire fortune of the lovers at the moment. Beauty laughingly suggested that her celebrated hair might prove worth the price of their dinner. The poet thought a pawn-broker might surely be found to advance ten shillings on his poem— the original MS. too—else had they nothing to pawn, save a few gold and silver dreams which they couldn't spare. What was to be done? Sell some books, of course! It made them shudder to think how many poets they had eaten in this fashion.

It was sheer cannibalism—but what was to be done! Their slender stock of books had been reduced entirely to poetry. If there had only been a philosopher or a modern novelist, the sacrifice wouldn't have seemed so unnatural. And then Beauty's eyes fell upon a very fat informing-looking volume on the poet's desk.

"Wouldn't this do?" she said.

"Why, of course!" he exclaimed; "the very thing. A new history of socialism just sent me for review. Hang the review; we want our dinner, don't we, little one? And then I've read the preface, and looked through the index—quite enough to make a column of—with a plentiful supply of general principles thrown in! Why, of course, there's our dinner, for certain, dull and indigestible as it looks. It's worth fifty minor poets at old Moser's. Come along. . . ."

So off went the happy pair—ah! how much happier was Beauty than ever so many fine ladies one knows who have only, so to say, to rub their wedding-rings for a banquet to rise out of the ground, with the most distinguished guests around the table, champagne of the best, and conversation of the worst.

Old Moser found histories of socialism profitable, more profitable perhaps than socialism, and he actually gave five-and-six-pence for the volume. With the ninepence already in their pockets, you will see that they were now possessors of quite a small fortune. Six-and-three-pence! it wouldn't pay for one's lunch nowadays. Ah! but that is because the poor alone know the art of dining.

You needn't wish to be much happier and merrier than those two lovers, as they gaily hastened to that bright and cosy corner of the town where those lovely ham-and-beef shops make glad the faces of the passers-by. O those hams with their honest shining faces, polished like mahogany—and the man inside so happy all day slicing them with those wonderful long knives (which, of course, the superior class of reader has never seen) worn away to a veritable thread, a mere wire, but keen as Excalibur. Beauty used to calculate in her quaint way how much steel was worn away with each pound of ham, and how much therefore went to the sandwich. And what an artist was the carver! What a true eye, what a firm flexible wrist—never a shaving of fat too much—he was too great an artist for that. Then there were those dear little cream cheeses and those little brown jugs of yellow cream, come all the way from Devonshire— you could hear the cows lowing across the rich pasture, and hear the milkmaids singing and the milk whizzing into the pail, as you looked at them.

And then those perfectly lovely sausages—I beg the reader's pardon! I forgot that the very mention of the word smacks of vulgarity. Yet, all the same, I venture to think that a secret taste for sausages among the upper classes is more widespread than we have any idea of. I confess that Beauty and her poet were at first ashamed of admitting their vulgar frailty to each other. They needed to know each other very well first. Yet there is nothing, when once confessed, that brings two people so close as—a taste for sausages!

"You darling!" exclaimed Beauty with something like tears in her voice, when her poet first admitted this touch of nature—and then next moment they were in fits of laughter that a common taste for a very "low" food should bring tears to their eyes! But such are the vagaries of love—as you will know, if you know anything about it—"vulgar," no doubt, though only the vulgar would so describe them—for it is only vulgarity that is always "refined"!

Then there was the florist's to visit. What beautiful trades some people ply! To sell flowers is surely like dealing in fairies. Beautiful must grow the hands that wire them, and sweet the flower-girl's every thought.

There remained but the wine-merchant's, or, had we not better say at once, the grocer's, for our lovers could afford no rarer vintages than Tintara or the golden burgundy of Australia; and it is wonderful to think what a sense of festivity those portly colonial flagons lent to their little dining-table. Sometimes, I may confide, when they wanted to feel very dissipated, and were very rich, they would allow themselves a small bottle of Benedictine—and you should have seen Beauty's eyes as she luxuriously sipped at her green little liqueur glass, for, like most innocent people, she enjoyed to the full the delight of feeling occasionally wicked. However, these were rare occasions, and this night was not one of them.

Half a pound of black grapes completed their shopping, and then, with their arms full of their purchases, they made their way home again, the two happiest people in what is, after all, a not unhappy world.

Then came the cooking and the laying of the table. For all her Leonardo face, Beauty was a great cook—like all good women, she was as earthly in some respects as she was heavenly in others, which I hold to be a wise combination—and, indeed, both were excellent cooks; and the poet was unrivalled at "washing up," which, I may say, is the only skeleton at these Bohemian feasts.

You should have seen the gusto with which Beauty pricked those sausages—I had better explain to the un-Bohemian reader that to attempt to cook a sausage without first pricking it vigorously with a fork, to allow for the expansion of its juicy gases, is like trying to smoke a cigar without first cutting off the end—and O, to hear again their merry song as they writhed in torment in the hissing pan, like Christian martyrs raising hymns of praise from the very core of Smithfield fires. Meanwhile, the poet would be surpassing himself in the setting-out of the little table, cutting up the bread reverently as though it were for an altar—as indeed it was—studying the effect of the dish of tomatoes now at this corner, now at that, arranging the flowers with even more care than he arranged the adjectives in his sonnets, and making ever so sumptuous an effect with that half-a-pound of grapes.

And then at last the little feast would begin, with a long grace of eyes meeting and hands clasping; true eyes that said "how good it is to behold you, to be awake together in this dream of life "; true hands that said "I will hold you fast for ever—not death even shall pluck you from my hand, shall loose this bond of you and me"; true eyes, true hands, that had immortal meanings far beyond the speech of mortal words.

And it had all come out of that dull history of socialism, and had cost little more than a crown! What lovely things can be made out of money! Strange to think that a little silver coin of no possible use or beauty in itself can be exchanged for so much tangible beautiful pleasure. A piece of money is like a piece of opium, for in it lie locked up the most wonderful dreams—if you have only the brains and hearts to dream them.

When at last the little feast grew near its end, Love and Beauty would smoke their cigarettes together; and it was a favourite trick of theirs to lower the lamp a moment, so that they might see the stars rush down upon them through the skylight which hung above their table. It gave them a sense of great sentinels, far away out in the lonely universe, standing guard over them, that seemed to say their love was safe in the tender keeping of great forces. They were poor, but then they had the stars and the flowers and the great poets for their servants and friends—and, best of all, they had each other. Do you call that being poor?

And then, in the corner, stood that magical box with the ivory keys, whose strings waited ready night and day—strange media through which the myriad voices, the inner-sweet thoughts, of the great world-soul found speech, messengers of the stars to the heart, and of the heart to the stars.

Beauty's songs were very simple. She got little practice, for her poet only cared to have her sing over and over again the same sweet songs; and perhaps if you had heard her sing "Ask nothing more of me, sweet," or "Darby and Joan," you would have understood his indifference to variety.

At last the little feast is quite, quite finished. Beauty has gone home; her lover still carries her face in his heart as she waved and waved and waved to him from the rattling lighted tramcar; long he sits and sits thinking of her, gazing up at those lonely ancient stars; the air is still bright with her presence, sweet with her thoughts, warm with her kisses, and as he turns to the shut piano, he can still see her white hands on the keys and her girlish face raised in an ecstasy—Beata Beatrix—above the music.

"O love, my love! if I no more should see
Thyself, nor on the earth the shadow of thee,
Nor image of thine eyes in any spring—
How then should sound upon Life's darkening slope
The ground-whirl of the perished leaves of Hope,
The wind of Death's imperishable wing?"

And then . . . . he would throw himself upon his bed, and burst into tears.

"And they are gone: ay, ages long ago
These lovers fled away into the storm."

That seventh-story heaven once more leads a dull life as the office of a ship-chandler, and harsh voices grate the air where Beauty sang. The books and the flowers and the lovers' faces are gone for ever. I suppose the stars are the same, and perhaps they sometimes look down through that roof-window, and wonder what has become of those two lovers who used to look up at them so fearlessly long ago.

But friends of mine who believe in God say that He has given His angels charge concerning that dingy old seventh-floor heaven, and that, for those who have eyes to see, there is no place where a great dream has been dreamed that is not thus watched over by the guardian angels of memory.

For M. Le G., a Birthday Present; 25 September, 1895.

Three Stories

I—A Poet in the City

"In the midway of this our mortal life,
I found me in a gloomy wood, astray."

I (and when I say I, I must be understood to be speaking dramatically) I only venture into the City once a year, for the very pleasant purpose of drawing that twelve-pound-ten by which the English nation, ever so generously sensitive to the necessities, not to say luxuries, of the artist, endeavours to express its pride and delight in me. It would be a very graceful exercise of gratitude for me here to stop and parenthesise the reader on the subject of all that twelve-pound-ten has been to me, how it has quite changed the course of my life, given me that long-desired opportunity of doing my best work in peace, for which so often I vainly sighed in Fleet Street, and even allowed me an indulgence in minor luxuries which I could not have dreamed of enjoying before the days of that twelve-pound-ten. Now not only peace and plenty, but leisure and luxury are mine. There is nothing goes so far as—Government money.

Usually on these literally State occasions, I drive up in state, that is in a hansom. There is only one other day in the year in which I am so splendid, but that is another beautiful story. It, too, is a day and an hour too joyous to be approached otherwise than on winged wheels, too stately to be approached in merely pedestrian fashion. To go on foot to draw one's pension seems a sort of slight on the great nation that does one honour, as though a Lord Mayor should make his appearance in the procession in his office coat.

So I say it is my custom to go gaily, and withal stately, to meet my twelve-pound-ten in a hansom. For many reasons the occasion always seems something of an adventure, and I confess I always feel a little excited about it, indeed, to tell the truth, a little nervous As I glide along in my state barge (which seems a much more proper and impressive image for a hansom than "gondola," with its reminiscences of Earl's Court) I feel like some fragile country flower torn from its roots, and bewilderingly hurried along upon the turbid, swollen stream of London life.

The stream glides sweetly with a pleasant trotting tinkle of bells by the green park -side of Piccadilly, and sweet is it to hear the sirens singing and to see them combing their gilded locks on the yellow sands of Piccadilly Circus—so called, no doubt, from the number of horses and the skill of their drivers. Here are the whirling pools of pleasure, merry wheels of laughing waters, where your hansom glides along with a golden ease—it is only when you enter the First Cataract of the Strand that you become aware of the far-distant terrible roar of the Falls! They are yet nearly two miles away, but already, like Niagara, thou hearest the sound thereof—the fateful sound of that human Niagara, where all the great rivers of London converge: the dark, strong floods surging out from the gloomy fastnesses of the East End, the quick-running streams from the palaces of the West, the East with its waggons, the West with its hansoms, the four winds with their omnibuses, the horses and carriages under the earth jetting up their companies of grimy passengers, the very air busy with a million errands.

You are in the rapids, metaphorically speaking, as you crawl down Cheapside, and there where the Bank of England and the Mansion House rise sheer and awful from, shall we say, this boiling cauldron, this "hell" of angry meeting waters—Threadneedle Street and Cornhill, Queen Victoria Street and Cheapside, each "running," again metaphorically, "like a mill race"—here in this wild maelstrom of human life and human conveyances, here is the true "Niagara in London," here are the most wonderful falls in the world—the London Falls.

"Yes!" I said softly to myself, and I could see the sly, sad smile on the face of the dead poet, at the thought of whose serene wisdom a silence like snow seemed momentarily to cover up the turmoil— "Yes!" I said softly, "there is still the same old crush at the corner of Fenchurch Street!"

By this time I had disbursed one of my two annual cab fares, and was standing a little forlorn at that very corner. It was a March afternoon, bitter and gloomy; lamps were already popping alight in a desolate way, and the east wind whistled mournfully through the ribs of the passers-by. A very unflower-like man was dejectedly calling out "daffodowndillies" close by. The sound of the pretty old word thus quaintly spoken, brightened the air better than the electric lights which suddenly shot rows of wintry moonlight along the streets. I bought a bunch of the poor, pinched flowers, and asked the man how he came to call them "daffodown-dillies."

"D'vunshire," he said, in anything but a Devonshire accent, and then the east wind took him and he was gone—doubtless to a neighbouring tavern; and no wonder, poor soul. Flowers certainly fall into strange hands here in London.

Well, it was nearing four, and if I wanted a grateful country's twelve-pound-ten, I must make haste—so presently I found myself in a great hall, of which I have no clearer impression than that there were soft little lights all about me, and a soft chime of falling gold, like the rippling of Pactolus. I have a sort of idea, too, of a great number of young men with most beautiful moustaches, playing with golden shovels—and as I thus stood among the soft lights and listened to the most beautiful sound in the world, I thought that thus must Danae have felt as she stood amid the falling shower. But I took care to see that my twelve sovereigns and a half were right number and weight for all that.

Once more in the street, I lingered awhile to take a last look at the Falls. What a masterful, alien life it all seemed to me. No single personality could hope to stand alone amid all that stress of ponderous, bullying forces. Only public companies and such great impersonalities could hope to hold their own, to swim in such a whirlpool and even they, I had heard whisper, far away in my quiet starlit garret, sometimes went down. "How," I cried," would—

"... my tiny spark of being wholly vanish in your deeps and heights . . .
Rush of suns, and roll of systems, and your fiery clash of meteorites,"

again quoting poetry. I always quote poetry in the City, as a protest—moreover, it clears the air.

The more people buffeted against me the more I felt this crushing sense of almost cosmic forces. Everybody was so plainly an atom in a public company, a drop of water in a tyrannous stream of human energy—companies that cared nothing for their individual atoms, streams that cared nothing for their component drops; such atoms and drops, for the most part to be had for thirty shillings a week. These people about me seemed no more like individual men and women than individual puffs in a mighty rushing wind, or the notes in a great scheme of music, are men and women—to the banker so many pens with ears whereon to perch them, to the capitalist so many "hands," and to the City man generally so many "helpless pieces of the game he plays" up there in spidery nooks and corners of the City.

As I listened to the throbbing of the great human engines in the buildings about me, a rising and a falling there seemed as of those great steel -limbed monsters, weird contortionists of metal, that jet up and down, and writhe and wrestle this way and that behind the long glass windows of great water-towers, or toil like Vulcan in the bowels of mighty ships—an expression of frenzy seems to come up even from the dumb tossing steel, sometimes it seems to be shaking great knuckled fists at one and brandishing threatening arms, as it strains and sweats beneath the lash of the compulsive steam. As one watches it there seems something of human agony about its panic-stricken labours, and something like a sense of pity surprises one—a sense of pity that anything in the world should have to work like that, even steel, even, as we say, senseless steel. What, then, of these great human engine houses! Will the engines always consent to rise and fall, night and day, like that? or will there some day be a mighty convulsion, and this blind Samson of labour pull down the whole engine-house upon his oppressors? Who knows? These are questions for great politicians and thinkers to decide, not for a poet, who is too much terrified by these forces to be able calmly to estimate and prophesy concerning them.

Yes! if you want to realise Tennyson's picture of "one poor Poet's scroll" ruling the world, take your poet's scroll down to Fenchurch Street and try it there. Ah, what a powerless little "private interest" seems poetry there, poetry "whose action is no stronger than a flower." In days of peace it ventures even into the morning papers, but let only a rumour of war be heard and it vanishes like a dream on doomsday morning. A County Council Election passeth over it and it is gone.

Yet it was near this very spot that Keats dug up the buried beauty of Greece, lying hidden beneath Finsbury Pavement! and in the deserted City churches great dramatists lie about us. Maybe I have wronged the City—and at this thought I remembered a little bookshop but a few yards away, blossoming like a rose right in the heart of the wilderness.

Here, after all, in spite of all my whirlpools and engine-houses, was for me the greatest danger in the City. Need I say, therefore, that I promptly sought it, hovered about it a moment—and entered. How much of that grateful governmental twelve-pound-ten came out alive, I dare not tell my dearest friend.

At all events I came out somehow reassured, more rich in faith. There was a might of poesy after all. There were words in the little yellow-leaved garland, nestling like a bird in my hand, that would outlast the bank yonder, and outlive us all. I held it up. How tiny it seemed, how frail amid all this stone and iron. A mere flower—a flower from the seventeenth century—long-lived for a flower! Yes, an immortelle.

II—Variations upon Whitebait

A very Pre-Raphaelite friend of mine came to me one day and said apropos of his having designed a very Early English chair: "After all, if one has anything to say one might as well put it into a chair!"

I thought the remark rather delicious, as also his other remark when one day in a curiosity-shop we were looking at another chair, which the dealer declared to be Norman. My friend seated himself in it very gravely, and after softly moving about from side to side, testing it, it would appear, by the sensation it imparted to the sitting portion of his limbs, he solemnly decided "I don t think the flavour of this chair is Norman!"

I thought of this Pre-Raphaelite brother as the Sphinx and I were seated a few evenings ago at our usual little dinner, in our usual little sheltered corner, on the Lover's Gallery of one of the great London restaurants. The Sphinx says that there is only one place in Europe where one can really dine, but as it is impossible to be always within reasonable train service of that Montsalvat of cookery, she consents to eat with me—she cannot call it dine—at the restaurant of which I speak. I being very simple-minded, untravelled, and unlanguaged, think it, in my Cockney heart, a very fine place indeed, with its white marble pillars surrounding the spacious peristyle, and flashing with a thousand brilliant lights and colours; with its stately cooks, clothed in white samite, mystic, wonderful, ranged behind a great altar loaded with big silver dishes, and the sacred musicians of the temple ranged behind them—while in and out go the waiters clothed in white and black, waiters so good and kind that I am compelled to think of Elijah being waited on by angels.

They have such an eye for a romance, too, and really take it personally to heart if it should befall that our little table is usurped by others that know not love. I like them, too, because they really seem to have an eye for the strange beauty and charm of the Sphinx, quite an unexpected taste for Botticelli. They ill conceal their envy of my lot, and sometimes in the meditative pauses between the courses I see them romantically reckoning how it might be possible by desperately saving up, by prodigious windfalls of tips, from unexampled despatch and sweetness in their ministrations, how it might be possible in ten years time, perhaps even in five—the lady would wait five years! and her present lover could be artistically poisoned meanwhile!—how it might be possible to come and sue for her beautiful hand. Then a harsh British cry for "waiter" comes like a rattle and scares away that beautiful dream-bird, though, as the poor dreamer speeds on the quest of roast beef for four, you can see it still circling with its wonderful blue feathers around his pomatumed head.

Ah, yes, the waiters know that the Sphinx is no ordinary woman. She cannot conceal even from them the mystical star of her face; they too catch far echoes of the strange music of her brain; they too grow dreamy with dropped hints of fragrance from the rose of her wonderful heart.

How reverently do they help her doff her little cloak of silk and lace; with what a worshipful inclination of the head, as in the presence of a deity, do they await her verdict of choice between rival soups shall—it be "clear or thick"? And when she decides on "thick" how relieved they seem to be, as if—well, some few matters remain undecided in the universe, but never mind, this is settled for ever, no more doubts possible on one portentous issue, at any rate—Madame will take her soup "thick."

"On such a night" our talk fell upon whitebait.

As the Sphinx's silver fork rustled among the withered silver upon her plate, she turned to me and said:

"Have you ever thought what beautiful little things these whitebait are?"

"Oh, yes," I replied, "they are the daisies of the deep sea, the threepenny-pieces of the ocean."

"You dear!" said the Sphinx, who is alone in the world in thinking me awfully clever. "Go on, say something else, something pretty about whitebait—there's a subject for you!"

Then it was that, fortunately, I remembered my Pre-Raphaelite friend, and I sententiously remarked: "Of course, if one has anything to say one cannot do better than say it about whitebait. . . . Well, whitebait. . . ."

But here, providentially, the band of the beef—that is, the band behind the beef; that is, the band that nightly hymns the beef (the phrase is to be had in three qualities)—struck up the overture from "Tannhäuser," which is not the only music that makes the Sphinx forget my existence; and thus, forgetting me, she momentarily forgot the whitebait. But I remembered, remembered hard—worked at pretty things, as metal-workers punch out their flowers of brass and copper. The music swirled about us like golden waves, in which swam myriad whitebait, like showers of tiny stars, like falling snow. To me it was one grand processional of whitebait, silver ripples upon streams of gold.

The music stopped. The Sphinx turned to me with the soul of Wagner in her eyes, and then she turned to the waiter: "Would it be possible," she said, "to persuade the bandmaster to play that wonderful thing over again?"

The waiter seemed a little doubtful, even for the Sphinx, but he went off to the bandmaster with the air of a man who has at last an opportunity to show that he can dare all for love. Personally, I have a suspicion that he poured his month's savings at the bandmaster's feet, and begged him to do this thing for the most wonderful lady in the world; or perhaps the bandmaster was really a musician, and his musician's heart was touched—lonely there amid the beef—to think that there was really some one, invisible though she were to him, some shrouded silver presence, up there among the beefeaters, who really loved to hear great music.

Perhaps it was thus made a night he has never forgotten; perhaps it changed the whole course of his life—who knows? The sweet reassuring request may have come to him at a moment when, sick of heart, he was deciding to abandon real music for ever, and settle down amid the beef and the beef-music of Old England.

Well, however, it was the waiter came back radiant with a Yes on every shining part of him, and if the "Tannhäuser" had been played well at first, certainly the orchestra surpassed themselves this second time.

When the great jinnee of music had once more passed out of the hall, the Sphinx turned with shining eyes to the waiter:

"Take," she said, "take these tears to the bandmaster. He has indeed earned them."

Tears, little one," I said. "See how they swim like whitebait in the fishpools of your eyes!"

"Oh, yes, the whitebait," rejoined the Sphinx, glad of a subject to hide her emotion. "Now tell me something nice about them, though the poor little things have long since disappeared. Tell me, for instance, how they get their beautiful little silver waterproofs?"

"Electric Light of the World," I said, "it is like this. While they are still quite young and full of dreams, their mother takes them out in picnic parties of a billion or so at a time to where the spring moon is shining, scattering silver from its purse of pearl far over the wide waters, silver, silver, for every little whitebait that cares to swim and pick it up. The mother, who has a contract with some such big restaurateur as ours here, chooses a convenient area of moonlight, and then at a given sign they all turn over on their sides, and bask and bask in the rays, little fin pressed lovingly against little fin—for this is the happiest time in the young whitebait's life: it is at these silvering parties that matches are made and future consignments of whitebait arranged for. Well, night after night, they thus lie in the moonlight, first on one side then on the other, till by degrees, tiny scale by scale, they have become completely lunar-plated. Ah! how sad they are when the end of that happy time has come."

"And what happens to them after that?" asked the Sphinx.

"One night when the moon is hidden their mother comes to them with treacherous wile, and suggests that they should go off on a holiday again to seek the moon—the moon that for a moment seems captured by the pearl-fishers of the sky. And so off they go merrily, but, alas, no moon appears, and presently they are aware of unwieldly bumping presences upon the surface of the sea, presences as of huge dolphins, and rough voices call across the water, till, scared, the little whitebaits turn home in flight—to find themselves somehow meshed in an invisible prison, a net as fine and strong as air, into which, O agony, they are presently hauled, lovely banks of silver, shining like opened coffers beneath the coarse and ragged flares of yellow torches. The rest is silence."

"What sad little lives! and what a cruel world it is!" said the Sphinx—as she crunched with her knife through the body of a lark, that but yesterday had been singing in the blue sky. Its spirit sang just above our heads as she ate, and the air was thick with the grey ghosts of all the whitebait she had eaten that night. But there were no longer any tears in her eyes.

III—A Seaport in the Moon

No one is so hopelessly wrong about the stars as the astronomer, and I trust that you never pay any attention to his remarks on the moon. He knows as much about the moon as a coiffeur knows of the dreams of the fair lady whose beautiful neck he makes still more beautiful. There is but one opinion upon the moon—namely, our own. And if you think that science is thus wronged, reflect a moment upon what science makes of things near at hand. Love, it says, is merely a play of pistil and stamen, our most fascinating poetry and art is "degeneration," and human life, generally speaking, is sufficiently explained by the "carbon compounds"—God-a-mercy! If science makes such grotesque blunders about radiant matters right under its nose, how can one think of taking its opinion upon matters so remote as the stars or even the moon, which is comparatively near at hand?

Science says that the moon is a dead world, a cosmic ship littered with the skeletons of its crew, and from which every rat of vitality has long since escaped. It is the ghost that rises from its tomb, every night to haunt its faithless lover, the world. It is a country of ancient silver mines, unworked for centuries. You may see the gaping mouths of the dark old shafts through your telescopes. You may even see the rusting pit tackle, the ruinous engine-houses, and the idle pick and shovel. Or you may say that it is counterfeit silver, coined to take in the young fools who love to gaze upon it. It is, so to speak, a bad half-a-crown.

As you will! but I am of Endymion's belief—and no one was ever more intimate with the moon. For me the moon is a country of great seaports, whither all the ships of our dreams come home. From all quarters of the world, every day of the week, there are ships sailing to the moon. They are the ships that sail just when and where you please. You take your passage on that condition. And it is ridiculous to think for what a trifle the captain will take you on so long a journey. If you want to come back, just to take an excursion and no more, just to take a lighted look at those coasts of rose and pearl, he will ask no more than a glass or two of bright wine; indeed, when the captain is very kind, a flower will take you there and back in no time; if you want to stay whole days there, but still come back dreamy and strange, you may take a little dark root and smoke it in a silver pipe, or you may drink a little phial of poppy-juice, and thus you shall find the Land of Heart's Desire; but if you are wise and would stay in that land forever, the terms are even easier: a little powder shaken into a phial of water, a little piece of lead no bigger than a pea and a farthing's worth of explosive fire, and thus also you are in the Land of Heart's Desire for ever.

I dreamed last night that I stood on the blustering windy wharf, and the dark ship was there. It was impatient, like all of us, to leave the world. Its funnels belched black smoke, its engines throbbed against the quay like arms that were eager to strike and be done, and a bell was beating impatient summons to be gone. The dark captain stood ready on the bridge, and he looked into each of our faces as we passed on board. "Is it for the long voyage?" he said. "Yes! the long voyage," I said—and his stern eyes seemed to soften as I answered.

At last we were all aboard, and in the twinkling of an eye were out of sight of land. Yet, once afloat, it seemed as though we should never reach our port in the moon—so it seemed to me as I lay awake in my little cabin, listening to the patient thud and throb of the great screws, beating in the ship's side like a human heart.

Talking with my fellow-voyagers, I was surprised to find that we were not all volunteers. Some in fact complained pitifully. They had, they said, been going about their business a day or two before, and suddenly a mysterious captain had laid hold of them, and pressed them to sail this unknown sea. Thus, without a word of warning, they had been compelled to leave behind them all they held dear. This one felt was a little hard of the captain; but those of us whose position was exactly the reverse, who had friends on the other side, all whose hopes indeed were invested there, were too selfishly expectant of port to be severe on the captain who was taking us thither.

There were three friends I had especially set out to see: two young lovers who had emigrated to those colonies in the moon just after their marriage, and there was another. What a surprise it would be to all three, for I had written no letter to say I was coming. Indeed, it was just a sudden impulse, the pistol flash of a long desire.

I tried to imagine what the town would be like in which they were now living. I asked the captain, and he answered with a sad smile, that it would be just exactly as I cared to dream it.

"O, well then," I thought, "I know what it will be like. There shall be a great restless, tossing estuary, with Atlantic winds for ever ruffling the sails of busy ships, ships coming home with laughter, ships leaving home with sad sea-gull cries of farewell. And the shaggy tossing water shall be bounded on either bank with high granite walls, and on one bank shall be a fretted spire soaring with a jangle of bells, from amid a tangle of masts, and underneath the bells and the masts shall go streets rising up from the strand, streets full of faces, and sweet with the smell of tar and the sea. O, captain, will it be morning or night when we come to my city? In the morning my city is like a sea-blown rose, in the night it is bright as a sailor's star.

"If it be early morning, what shall I do? I will run to the house in which my friends lie in happy sleep, never to be parted again, and kiss my hand to their shrouded window; and then I will run on and on till the city is behind and the sweetness of country lanes is about me, and I will gather flowers as I run, from sheer wantonness of joy, and then at last, flushed and breathless, I will stand beneath her window. I shall stand and listen, and I shall hear her breathing right through the heavy curtains, and the hushed garden and the sleeping house will bid me keep silence, but I shall cry a great cry up to the morning star, and say, No, I will not keep silence. Mine is the voice she listens for in her sleep. She will wake again for no voice but mine. Dear one, awake, the morning of all mornings has come!'"

As I write, the moon looks down at me like a Madonna from the great canvas of the sky. She seems beautiful with the beauty of all the eyes that have looked up at her, sad with all the tears of all those eyes; like a silver bowl brimming with the tears of dead lovers she seems. Yes, there are seaports in the moon, there are ships to take us there.

I—The Answer of the Rose

The Sphinx and I sat in our little box at Romeo and Juliet. It was the first time she had seen that fairy-tale of passion upon the stage. I had seen it played once before in Paradise. Therefore, I rather trembled to see it again in an earthly play-house, and as much as possible kept my eyes from the stage. All I knew of the performance but how much was that! was two lovely voices making love like angels; and when there were no words, the music told me what was going on. Love speaks so many languages.

One might as well look. It was as clear as moonlight to the tragic eye within the heart. The Sphinx was gazing on it all with those eyes that will never grow old, neither for years nor tears; but though I seemed to be seeing nothing but an advertisement of Paderewski pianos on the programme, I saw it O didn't I see it? all. The house had grown dark, and the music low and passionate, and for a moment no one was speaking. Only, deep in the thickets of my heart, there sang a tragic nightingale that, happily, only I could hear; and I said to myself, "Now the young fool is climbing the orchard wall! Yes, there go Benvolio and Mercutio calling him; and now he jests at scars who never felt a wound the other young fool is coming out on the balcony. God help them both! They have no eyes—no eyes or surely they would see the shadow that sings Love! Love! Love! like a fountain in the moonlight, and then shrinks away to chuckle Death! Death! Death! in the darkness!"

But, soft, what light from yonder window breaks!

The Sphinx turned to me for sympathy this time it was the soul of Shakespeare in her eyes.

"Yes!" I whispered; "it is the Opening of the Eternal Rose, sung by the Eternal Nightingale!"

She pressed my hand approvingly, and while the lovely voices made their heavenly love, I slipped out my silver-bound pocket-book of ivory, and pressed within it the rose which had just fallen from my lips.

The worst of a great play is that one is so dull between the acts. Wit is sacrilege, and sentiment is bathos. Not another rose fell from my lips during the performance, though that I minded little, as I was the more able to count the pearls that fell from the Sphinx's eyes.

It took quite half a bottle of champagne to pull us up to our usual spirits, as we sat at supper at a window where we could see London spread out beneath us like a huge black velvet flower, dotted with fiery embroideries, sudden flaring stamens, and rows of ant-like fireflies moving in slow zig-zag processions along and across its petals.

"How strange it seems," said the Sphinx, "to think that for every two of those moving double-lights, which we know to be the eyes of hansoms, but which seem up here nothing but gold dots in a very barbaric pattern of black and gold, there are two human beings, no doubt at this time of night two lovers, throbbing with the joy of life, and dreaming, heaven knows, what dreams!"

"Yes," I rejoined; "and to them I'm afraid we are even more impersonal. From their little Piccadilly coracles our watch-tower in the skies is merely a radiant facade of glowing windows, and no one of all who glide by realises that the spirited illumination is every bit due to your eyes. You have but to close them, and everyone will be asking what has gone wrong with the electric light."

A little nonsense is a great healer of the heart, and by means of such nonsense as this we grew merry again. And anon we grew sentimental and poetic, but thank heaven! we were no longer tragic.

Presently I had news for the Sphinx. "The rose-tree that grows in the garden of my mind," I said, "desires to blossom."

"May it blossom indeed," she replied; "for it has been flowerless all this long evening; and bring me a rose fresh with all the dews of inspiration no florist's flower, wired and artificially scented, no bloom of yesterday's hard-driven brains."

" I was only thinking," I said, "and apropos of nightingales and roses, that though all the world has heard the song of the nightingale to the rose, only the nightingale has heard the answer of the rose. You know what I mean?"

"Know what you mean? Of course that's always easy enough," retorted the Sphinx, who knows well how to be hard on me.

"I'm so glad," I ventured to thrust back; "for lucidity is the first success of expression: to make others see clearly what we ourselves are struggling to see, believe with all their hearts what we are just daring to hope, is well, the religion of a literary man?"

"Yes! It's a pretty idea," said the Sphinx, once more pressing the rose of my thought to her brain; "and indeed it's more than pretty . . ."

"Thank you!" I said humbly.

"Yes, it's true and many a humble little rose will thank you for it. For, your nightingale is a self-advertising bird. He never sings a song without an eye on the critics, sitting up there in their stalls among the stars. He never, or seldom, sings a song for pure love, just because he must sing it or die. Indeed, he has a great fear of death, unless you will guarantee him immortality. But the rose, the trusting little earth-born rose, that must stay all her life rooted in one spot till some nightingale comes to choose her some nightingale whose song maybe has been inspired and perfected by a hundred other roses, which are at the moment pot-pourri, ah, the shy bosom-song of the rose . . ." Here the Sphinx paused, and added abruptly: "Well there is no nightingale worthy to hear it!" "It is true," I agreed, "O trusting, little earth-born rose!" "Do you know why the rose has thorns?" suddenly asked the Sphinx. Of course I knew; but I always respect a joke, particularly when it is but half-born humourists always prefer to deliver themselves, so I shook my head.

"To keep off the nightingales, of course," said the Sphinx, the tone of her voice holding in mocking solution the words "Donkey" and "Stupid," which I recognised and meekly bore. "What an excellent idea!" I said. "I never thought of it before. But don t you think it's a little unkind? For, after all, if there were no nightingales, one shouldn't hear so much about the rose; and there is always the danger that if the rose continues too painfully thorny, the nightingale may go off and seek, say, a more accommodating lily."

"I have no opinion of lilies," said the Sphinx.

"Nor have I," I answered soothingly, "I much prefer roses but ... but . . ."

"But what?"

"But well, I much prefer roses. Indeed I do."

"Rose of the World," I continued with sentiment, "draw in your thorns. I cannot bear them."

"Ah!" she answered eagerly, "that is just it. The nightingale that is worthy of the rose will not only bear, but positively love, her thorns. It is for that reason she wears them. The thorns of the rose properly understood are but the tests of the nightingale. The nightingale that is frightened of the thorns is not worthy of the rose of that you may be sure. . . ."

"I am not frightened of the thorns," I managed to interject.

"Sing then once more," she cried, "the Song of the Nightingale."

And it was thus I sang:

"O Rose of the World, a nightingale,
A Bird of the World am I,
I have loved all the world and sung all the world,
But I come to your side to die.

"Tired of the world, as the world of me,
I plead for your quiet breast,
I have loved all the world and sung all the world
But where is the nightingale's nest?

"In a hundred gardens I sung the rose,
Rose of the World, I confess
But for every rose I have sung before
I love you the more, not less.

"Perfect it grew by each rose that died,
Each rose that has died for you,
The song that I sing yea, tis no new song,
It is tried and so it is true.

"Petal or thorn, yea! I have no care,
So that I here abide,
Pierce me, my love, or kiss me, my love,
But keep me close to your side.

"I know not your kiss from your scorn, my love,
Your breast from your thorn, my rose,
And if you must kill me, well, kill me, my love,
But say twas the death I chose."

"Is it true?" asked the Rose.

"As I am a nightingale," I replied; and as we bade each other good-night, I whispered:

"When may I expect the Answer of the Rose?"

II—Spring by Parcel Post

"They've taken all the Spring from the country to the town Like the butter and the eggs and the milk from the cow . . ."

So began to jig and jingle my thoughts as in my letters and newspapers this morning I read, buried alive among the solitary fastnesses of the Surrey hills, the last news from town. The news I envied most was that spring had already reached London. "Now," ran a pretty article on spring fashions, "the sunshine makes bright the streets, and the flower-baskets, like huge bouquets, announce the gay arrival of spring." I looked up and out through my hillside window. The black ridge on the other side of the valley stood a grim wall of burnt heather against the sky which sky, like the bullets in the nursery rhyme, was made unmistakably of lead; a close rain was falling methodically, and, generally speaking, the world looked like a soaked mackintosh. It wasn't much like the gay arrival of spring, and grimly I mused on the advantages of life in town.

Certainly, it did seem hard, I reflected, that town should be ahead of us even in such a country matter as spring. Flower-baskets indeed! Why, we haven't as much as a daisy for miles around. It is true that on the terrace there the crocuses blaze like a street on fire, that the primroses thicken into clumps, lying among their green leaves like pounds of country butter; it is true that the blue cones of the little grape hyacinth are there, quaintly formal as a child's toy-flowers; yes! and the big Dutch hyacinths are already shamelessly enceinte with their buxom waxen blooms, so fat and fragrant (One is already delivered of a fine blossom. Well, that is a fine baby, to be sure! say the other hyacinths, with babes no less bonny under their own green aprons all waiting for the doctor sun). Then among the blue-green blades of the narcissus, here and there you see a stem topped with a creamish chrysalis-like envelope, from which will soon emerge a beautiful eye, rayed round with white wings, looking as though it were meant to fly, but remaining rooted a butterfly on a stalk; while all the beds are crowded with indeterminate beak and blade, pushing and elbowing each other for a look at the sun, which, however, sulkily declines to look at them. It is true there is spring on the terrace, but even so it is spring imported from the town spring bought in Holborn, spring delivered free by parcel post; for where would the terrace have been but for the city seedsman that magician who sends you strangely spotted beans and mysterious bulbs in shrivelled cerements, weird little flower-mummies that suggest centuries of forgotten silence in painted Egyptian tombs. This strange and shrivelled thing can surely never live again, we say, as we hold it in our hands, seeing not the glowing circles of colour, tiny rings of Saturn, packed so carefully inside this flower-egg, the folds of green and silver silk wound round and round the precious life within.

But, of course, this is all the seedsman's cunning, and no credit to Nature; and I repeat that were it not for railways and the parcel post goodness knows whether we should ever get any spring at all in the country! Think of the days when it had to travel down by stage-coach. For, left to herself, what is the best Nature can do for you with March well on the way? Personally, I find the face of the country practically unchanged. It is, to all intents and purposes, the same as it has been for the last three or four months as grim, as unadorned, as bleak, as draughty, and generally as comfortless as ever. There isn't a flower to be seen, hardly a bird worth listening to, not a tree that is not winter-naked, and not a chair to sit down upon. If you want flowers on your walks you must bring them with you; songs, you must take a poet under your arm; and if you want to rest, lean laboriously on your stick or take your chance of rheumatism.

Of course your specialists, your botanists, your nature detectives, will tell you otherwise. They have surprised a violet in the act of blossoming; after long and excited chase have discovered a clump of primroses in their wild state; seen one butterfly, heard one cuckoo. But as one swallow does not make a summer, it takes more than one cuckoo to make a spring. I confess that only yesterday I saw three sulphur butterflies, with my own eyes; I admit the catkins, and the silver-notched palm; and I am told on good colour-authority that there is a lovely purplish bloom, almost like plum-bloom, over certain copses in the valley j by taking thought, I have observed the long horizontal arms of the beech growing spurred with little forked branches of spear-shaped buds, and I see little green nipples pushing out through the wolf-coloured rind of the dwarf fir-trees. Spring is arming in secret to attack the winter that is sure enough, but spring in secret is no spring for me. I want to see her marching gaily with green pennons, and flashing sun-blades, and a good band.

I want butterflies as they have them at the Lyceum "butterflies all white," "butterflies all blue," "butterflies of gold," and I should particularly fancy "butterflies all black." But there, again, you see, you must go to town, within hearing of Mrs. Patrick Campbell's voix d'or. I want the meadows thickly inlaid with buttercups and daisies; I want the trees thick with green leaves, the sky all larks and sunshine; I want hawthorn and wild roses both at once; I want some go, some colour, some warmth in the world. O where are the pipes of Pan?

The pipes of Pan are in town, playing at street corners and in the centres of crowded circuses, piled high with flower-baskets blazing with refulgent flowery masses of white and gold. Here are the flowers you can only buy in town; simple flowers enough, but only to be had in town. Here are fragrant banks of violets every few yards, conflagrations of daffodils at every crossing, and narcissus in scented starry garlands for your hair.

You wander through the Strand, or along Regent Street, as through the meadows of Enna sweet scents, sweet sounds, sweet shapes, are all about you; the town-butterflies, white, blue, and gold, "wheel and shine" and flutter from shop to shop, suddenly resurgent from their winter wardrobes as from a chrysalis; bright eyes flash and flirt along the merry, jostling street, while the sun pours out his golden wine overhead, splashing it about from gilded domes and bright-faced windows and ever are the voices at the corners and the crossings calling out the sweet flower-names of the spring!

But here in the country it is still all rain and iron. I am tired of waiting for this slow-moving provincial spring. Let us to the town to meet the spring for:

"They've taken all the spring from the country to the town

Like the butter and the eggs and the milk from the cow;
And if you want a primrose, you write to London now,
And if you need a nightingale, well
Whiteley sends it down."

III—About the Securities

When I say that my friend Matthew lay dying, I want you so far as possible to dissociate the statement from any conventional, and certainly from any pictorial, conceptions of death which you may have acquired. Death sometimes shows himself one of those impersonal artists who conceal their art, and, unless you had been told, you could hardly have guessed that Matthew was dying, dying indeed sixty miles an hour, dying of consumption, dying because someone else had died four years before, dying too of debt.

Connoisseurs, of course, would have understood; at a glance, would have named the sculptor who was silently chiselling those noble hollows in the finely modelled face, that Pygmalion who turns all flesh to stone, at a glance would have named the painter who was cunningly weighting the brows with darkness that the eyes might shine the more with an unaccustomed light. Matthew and I had long been students of the strange wandering artist, had begun by hating his art (it is ever so with an art unfamiliar to us!) and had ended by loving it.

"Let us see what the artist has added to the picture since yesterday," said Matthew, signing to me to hand him the mirror.

"H'm," he murmured, "he's had one of his lazy days, I'm afraid. He's hardly added a touch just a little heightened the chiaroscuro, sharpened the nose a trifle, deepened some little the shadows round the eyes . . . ."

"O why," he presently sighed, "does he not work a little overtime and get it done? He's been paid handsomely enough . . . ."

"Paid," he continued, "by a life that is so much undeveloped gold-mine, paid by all my uncashed hopes and dreams . . . ."

"He works fast enough for me, old fellow," I interrupted, "there was a time, was there not, when he worked too fast for you and me?"

There are moments, for certain people, when such fantastic unreality as this is the truest realism. Matthew and I talked like this with our brains, because we hadn't the courage to allow our hearts to break in upon the conversation. Had I dared to say some real emotional thing, what effect would it have had but to set poor tired Matthew a-coughing? and it was our aim that he should die with as little to-do as practicable. The emotional in such situations is merely the obvious. There was no need for either of us to state the elementary feelings of our love. I knew that Matthew was going to die, and he knew that I was going to live; and we pitied each other accordingly, though I confess my feeling for him was rather one of envy, when it was not congratulation.

Thus, to tell the truth, we never mentioned "the hereafter." I don t believe it even occurred to us. Indeed, we spent the few hours that remained of our friendship in retailing the latest gathered of those good stones with which we had been accustomed to salt our intercourse.

One of Matthew's anecdotes was, no doubt, somewhat suggested by the occasion, and I should add that he had always somewhat of an ecclesiastical bias, would, I believe, have ended some day as a Monsignor, a notable "Bishop Blougram."

His story was of an evangelistic preacher who desired to impress his congregation with the unmistakable reality of hell-fire. "You know the Black Country, my friends," he had declaimed, "you have seen it, at night, flaring with a thousand furnaces, in the lurid incandescence of which, myriads of unhappy beings, our fellow-creatures (God forbid!) snatch a precarious existence, you have seen them silhouetted against the yellow glare, running hither and thither as it seemed from afar, in the very jaws of the awful fire. Have you realised that the burdens with which they thus run hither and thither are molten iron, iron to which such a stupendous heat has been applied that it has melted, melted as though it had been sugar in the sun well! returning to hell-fire, let me tell you this, that in hell they eat this fiery molten metal for ice-cream, yes! and are glad to get anything so cool."

It was thus we talked while Matthew lay dying, for why should we not talk as we had lived? We both laughed long and heartily over this story, perhaps it would have amused us less had Matthew not been dying; and then his kind old nurse brought in our lunch. We had both excellent appetites, and were far from indifferent to the dainty little meal which was to be our last but one together. I brought my table as close to Matthew's pillow as was possible, and he stroked my hand with tenderness in which there was a touch of gratitude.

"You are not frightened of the bacteria!" he laughed sadly, and then he told me, with huge amusement, how a friend (and a true dear friend for all that) had come to see him a day or two before, and had hung over the end of the bed to say farewell, daring to approach no nearer, mopping his fear-perspiring brows with a handkerchief soaked in "Eucalyptus"!

"He had brought an anticipatory elegy too," said my friend, "written against my burial. I wish you'd read it for me" and he fidgeted for it in the nervous manner of the dying, and, finding it among his pillows, handed it to me saying, "you needn't be frightened of it. It is well dosed with Eucalyptus."

We laughed even more over this poem than over our stories, and then we discussed the terms of three cremation societies to which, at the express request of my friend, I had written a day or two before.

Then having smoked a cigar and drunk a glass of port together (for the assured dying are allowed to "live well"), Matthew grew sleepy, and tucking him beneath the counterpane, I left him, for after all, he was not to die that day.

Circumstances prevented my seeing him again for a week. When I did so, entering the room poignantly redolent of the strange sweet odour of antiseptics, I saw that the great artist had been busy in my absence. Indeed, his work was nearly at end. Yet to one unfamiliar with his methods, there was still little to alarm in Matthew's face. In fact, with the exception of his brain, and his ice-cold feet, he was alive as ever. And even to his brain had come a certain unnatural activity, a life as of the grave, a sort of vampire vitality, which would assuredly have deceived anyone who had not known him. He still told his stories, laughed and talked with the same unconquerable humour, was in every way alert and practical, with this difference that he had forgotten he was going to die, and that the world in which he exercised his various faculties was another world to that in which, in spite of his delirium, we ate our last boiled fowl, drank our last wine, smoked our last cigar together. His talk was so convincingly rational, dealt with such unreal matters in so every day a fashion that you were ready to think that surely it was you and not he whose mind was wandering.

"You might reach that pocket-book, and ring for Mrs. Davies," he would say in so casual a way that of course you would ring. On Mrs. Davies's appearance he would be fumbling about among the papers in his pocket-book, and presently he would say, with a look of frustration that went to one's heart "I've got a ten pound note somewhere here for you, Mrs. Davies, to pay you up till Saturday, but somehow I seem to have lost it. Yet it must be somewhere about. Perhaps you'll find it as you make the bed in the morning. I'm so sorry to have troubled you. . . ."

And then he would grow tired and doze a little on his pillow.

Suddenly he would be alert again and with a startling vividness tell me strange stories from the dreamland into which he was now passing.

I had promised to see him on the Monday, but had been prevented, and had wired to him accordingly. This was Tuesday.

"You needn't have troubled to wire," he said. "Didn't you know I was in London from Saturday to Monday?"

"The doctor and Mrs. Davies didn't know," he continued with the creepy cunning of the dying, "I managed to slip away to look at a house I think of taking in fact I've taken it. It's in in now, where is it? Now isn't that silly? I can see it as plain as anything yet I cannot, for the life of me, remember where it is, or the number. ... It was somewhere St. John's Wood way . . . never mind, you must come and see me there, when we get in. . . ."

I said that he was dying in debt, and thus the heaven that lay about his deathbed was one of fantastic El dorados, sudden colossal legacies, and miraculous windfalls.

"I haven't told you," he said presently, "of the piece of good luck that has befallen me. You are not the only person in luck. I can hardly expect you to believe me, it sounds so like the Arabian nights. However, it's true for all that. Well, one of the little sisters was playing in the garden a few afternoons ago, making mud-pies or something of that sort, and she suddenly scraped up a sovereign. Presently she found two or three more, and our curiosity becoming aroused, a turn or two with the spade revealed quite a bed of gold, and the end of it was that on further excavating, the whole garden proved to be one mass of sovereigns. Sixty thousand pounds we counted .... and then what do you think it suddenly melted away . . . ."

He paused for a moment, and continued more in amusement than regret:

"Yes the government got wind of it, and claimed the whole lot as treasure-trove!"

"But not," he added slyly, "before I'd paid off two or three of my biggest bills. Yes and you'll keep it quiet, of course, there's another lot been discovered in the garden, but we shall take good care the government doesn't get hold of it this time, you may bet."

He told this wild story with such an air of simple conviction that, odd as it may seem, one believed every word of it. But the tale of his sudden good fortune was not ended.

"You've heard of old Lord Osterley," he presently began again. "Well, congratulate me, old man, he has just died and left everything to me. You know what a splendid library he had to think that that will all be mine and that grand old park through which we've so often wandered, you and I. Well, we shall need fear no gamekeeper now, and of course, dear old fellow, you'll come and live with me like a prince and just write your own books and say farewell to journalism forever. Of course I can hardly believe it's true yet. It seems too much of a dream, and yet there's no doubt about it. I had a letter from my solicitors this morning, saying that they were engaged in going through the securities and—and but the letter's somewhere over there, you might read it. No? can't you find it? It's there somewhere about I know. Never mind, you can see it again . . . ." he finished wearily.

"Yes!" he presently said, half to himself, "it will be a wonderful change! a wonderful change!"

At length the time came to say good-bye, a good-bye I knew must be the last, for my affairs were taking me so far away from him that I could not hope to see him for some days.

"I'm afraid, old man," I said, "that I mayn't be able to see you for another week."

"O never mind, old fellow, don't worry about me. I'm much better now and by the time you come again we shall know all about the securities."

The securities! My heart had seemed like a stone, incapable of feeling, all those last unreal hours together, but the pathos of that sad phrase, so curiously symbolic, suddenly smote it with over whelming pity, and the tears sprang to my eyes for the first time.

As I bent over him to kiss his poor damp forehead, and press his hand for the last farewell, I murmured:

"Yes dear, dear old friend. We shall know all about the securities."

IV—The Donkey that Loved a Star

"That is how the donkey tells his love!" I said one day, with intent to be funny, as the prolonged love-whoop of a distant donkey was heard in the land.

"Don't be too ready to laugh at donkeys," said my friend. "For," he continued, "even donkeys have their dreams. Perhaps, indeed, the most beautiful dreams are dreamed by donkeys."

"Indeed," I said, "and now that I think of it, I remember to have said that most dreamers are donkeys, though I never expected so scientific a corroboration of a fleeting jest."

Now my friend is an eminent scientist and poet in one, a serious combination, and he took my remarks with seriousness at once scientific and poetic.

"Yes," he went on, "that is where you clever people make a mistake. You think that because a donkey has only two vowel-sounds wherewith to express his emotions, he has no emotions to express. But let me tell you, sir. ..."

But here we both burst out laughing.

"You Golden Ass!" I said, "take a munch of these roses, perhaps they will restore you."

"No," he resumed, "I am quite serious. I have for many years past made a study of donkeys high-stepping critics call it the study of Human Nature however, it's the same thing and I must say that the more I study them the more I love them. There is nothing so well worth studying as the misunderstood, for the very reason that everybody thinks he understands it. Now, to take another instance, most people think they have said the last word on a goose when they have called it a goose! but let me tell you, sir. ..."

But here again we burst out laughing.

"Dear goose of the golden eggs," I said, "pray leave to discourse on geese to-night though lovely and pleasant would the discourse be to-night I am all agog for donkeys."

"So be it," said my friend, "and if that be so, I cannot do better than tell you the story of the donkey that loved a star keeping for another day the no less fascinating story of the goose that loved an angel."

By this time I was, appropriately, all ears.

"Well," he once more began, "there was once a donkey, quite an intimate friend of mine, and I have no friend of whom I am prouder, who was unpractically fond of looking up at the stars. He could go a whole day without thistles, if night would only bring him stars. Of course he suffered no little from his fellow-donkeys for this curious passion of his. They said well that it did not become him, for indeed it was no little laughable to see him gazing so sentimentally at the remote and pitiless heavens. Donkeys who belonged to Shakespeare Societies recalled the fate of Bottom, the donkey who had loved a fairy, but our donkey paid little heed. There is perhaps only one advantage in being a donkey namely, a hide impervious to criticism. In our donkey's case it was rather a dream that made him forget his hide a dream that drew up all the sensitiveness from every part, from hoof, and hide, and ears, so that all the feeling in his whole body was centred in his eyes and brain, and those, as we have said, were centred on a star. He took it for granted that his fellows should sneer and kick-out at him, it was ever so with genius among the donkeys, and he had very soon grown used to these attentions of his brethren, which were powerless to withdraw his gaze from the star he loved. For though he loved all the stars, as every individual man loves all women, there was one star he loved more than any other; and standing one midnight among his thistles, he prayed a prayer, a prayer that some day it might be granted him to carry that star upon his back which, he recalled, had been sanctified by the holy sign were it but for ever so short a journey. Just to carry it a little way, and then to die. This to him was a dream beyond the dreams of donkeys.

"Now, one night," continued my friend, taking breath for himself and me, "our poor donkey looked up to the sky, and lo! the star was nowhere to be seen. He had heard it said that stars sometimes fall. Evidently his star had fallen. Fallen! but what if it had fallen upon the earth? Being a donkey, the wildest dreams seemed possible to him. And, strange as it may seem, there came a day when a poet came to his master and bought our donkey to carry his little child. Now, the very first day he had her upon his back, the donkey knew that his prayer had been answered, and that the little swaddled babe he carried was the star he had prayed for. And, indeed, so it was, for so long as donkeys ask no more than to fetch and carry for their beloved, they may be sure of beauty upon their backs. Now, so long as this little girl that was a star remained a little girl, our donkey was happy. For many pretty years she would kiss his ugly muzzle and feed his mouth with sugar and thus our donkey's thoughts sweetened day by day, till from a natural pessimist he blossomed into a perfectly absurd optimist, and dreamed the donkiest of dreams. But one day, as he carried the girl who was really a star through the spring lanes, a young man walked beside her, and though our donkey thought very little of his talk in fact, felt his plain hee haw to be worth all its smart chirping and twittering yet it evidently pleased the maiden. It included quite a number of vowel-sounds, though if the maiden had only known, it didn't mean half so much as the donkey's plain monotonous declaration.

"Well, our donkey soon began to realise that his dream was nearing its end; and, indeed, one day his little mistress came bringing him the sweetest of kisses, the very best sugar in the very best shops, but for all that our donkey knew that it meant good-bye. It is the charming manner of English girls to be at their sweetest when they say good-bye.

"Our dreamer-donkey went into exile as servant to a wood cutter, and his life was lenient if dull, for the woodcutter had no sticks to waste upon his back; and next day his young mistress who was once a star took a pony for her love, whom some time after she discarded for a talented hunter, and, one fine day, like many of her sex, she pitched her affections upon a man he too being a talented hunter. To their wedding came all the countryside. And with the countryside came a donkey. He carried a great bundle of firewood for the servants hall, and as he waited outside, gazing up at his old loves the stars, while his master drank deeper and deeper within, he revolved many thoughts. But he is only known to have made one remark in the nature, one may think, or a grim jest.

"After all! he was heard to say, she has married a donkey, after all.

"No doubt it was feeble; but then our donkey was growing old and bitter, and hope deferred had made him a cynic."

Two Prose Fancies

I—The Silver Girl

Sometimes when I have thought that the Sphinx's mouth is cruel, and could not forget its stern line for all her soft eyes, I have reassured myself with the memory of a day when I saw it so soft and tender with heavenly pity that I could have gone down on my knees then and there by the side of the luncheon table, where the champagne was already cooling in the ice-pail, and worshipped her—would have done so had I thought such public worship to her taste. It was no tenderness to me, but that was just why I valued it. Tender she has been to me, and stern anon, as I have merited; but, would you understand the heart of woman, know if it be soft or hard, you will not trust her tenderness (or fear her sternness) to yourself; you will watch, with a prayer in your heart, for her tenderness to others.

She came late to our lunch that day, and explained that she had travelled by omnibus. As she said the word omnibus, for some reason as yet mysterious to me, I saw the northern lights I love playing in the heaven of her face. I wondered why, but did not ask as yet, delaying, that I might watch those fairy fires of emotion, for her face was indeed like a star of which a little child told me the other day. I think some one must have told him first, for as we looked through the window one starlit night, he communicated very confidentially that whenever any one in the world shed a tear of pure pity, God's angels caught it in lily-cups and carried it right up to heaven, and that when God had thus collected enough of them, he made them into a new star. "So," said the little boy, "there must have been a good deal of kind people in the world to cry all those stars."

It was of that story I thought as I said to the Sphinx:

"What is the matter, dear Madonna? Your face is the Star or Tears."

And then I ventured gently to tease her.

"What can have happened? No sooner did you speak the magic word 'omnibus,' than you were transfigured and taken from my sight in a silver cloud of tears. An omnibus does not usually awaken such tenderness, or call up northern lights to the face as one mentions it, ... though," I added wistfully, "one has met passengers to and from heaven in its musty corners, travelled life's journey with them a penny stage, and lost them for ever. . . ."

"So," I further ventured, "may you have seemed to some fortunate fellow-passenger, an accidental companion of your wonder, as from your yellow throne by the driver. . . ."

"Oh, do be quiet," she said, with a little flash of steel. "How can you be so flippant," and then, noting the champagne, she exclaimed with fervour: "No wine for me to day! It s heartless, it's brutal. All the world is heartless and brutal . . . how selfish we all are. Poor fellow! . . . I wish you could have seen his face!"

"I sincerely wish I could," I said; "for then I should no doubt have understood why the words 'omnibus' and 'champagne,' not unfamiliar words, should . . . well, make you look so beautiful."

"Oh, forgive me! Haven't I told you?" she said, as absent-mindedly she watched the waiter filling her glass with champagne.

"Well," she continued, "you know the something Arms, where the bus always stops a minute or so on its way from Kensington. I was on top, near the driver, and, while we waited, my neighbour began to peel an orange and throw the pieces of peel down on to the pavement. Suddenly a dreadful, tattered figure of a man sprang out of some corner, and, eagerly picking up the pieces of peel, began ravenously to eat them, looking up hungrily for more. Poor fellow! he had quite a refined, gentle face, and I shouldn't have been surprised to hear him quote Horace, after the manner of Stevenson's gentlemen in distress. I was glad to see that the others noticed him too. Quite a murmur of sympathy sprang up amongst us, and a penny or two rang on the pavement. But it was the driver who did the thing that made me cry. He was one of those prosperous young drivers, with beaver hats and smart overcoats, and he had just lit a most well-to-do cigar. With the rest of us he had looked down on poor Lazarus, and for a moment, but only for a moment, with a certain contempt. Then a wonderful kindness came into his face, and, next minute, he had done a great deed—he had thrown Lazarus his newly-lit cigar."

"Splendid!" I ventured to interject.

"Yes, indeed!" she continued; "and I couldn't help telling him so. ... But you should have seen the poor fellow's face as he picked it up. Evidently his first thought was that it had fallen by mistake, and he made as if to return it to his patron. It was an impossible dream that it could be for him—a mere rancid cigar-end had been a windfall, but this was practically a complete, unsmoked cigar. But the driver nodded reassuringly, and then you should have seen the poor fellow's joy. There was almost a look of awe, that such fortune should have befallen him, and tears of gratitude sprang into his eyes. Really, I don't exaggerate a bit. I'd have given anything for you to have seen him—though it was heart-breaking, that terrible look of joy, such tragic joy. No look of misery or wretchedness could have touched one like that. Think how utterly, abjectly destitute one must be for a stranger's orange-peel to represent dessert, and an omnibus-driver's cigar set us crying for joy. . . ."

"Gentle heart," I said. "I fear poor Lazarus did not keep his cigar for long. . . ."

"But why? . . ."

"Why? Is it not already among the stars, carried up by those angels who catch the tears of pity, and along with Uncle Toby's 'damn,' and such bric-a-brac, in God's museum of fair deeds? We shall see it shining down on us as the stars come out to-night. Yes! that will be a pretty astronomical theory to exchange with the little boy who told me that the stars are made of tears. Some are made of tears, I shall say, but some are the glowing ends of newly lit cigars, thrown down by good omnibus-drivers to poor? starving fellows who haven't a bed to sleep in, nor a dinner to eat, nor a heart to love them, and not even a single cigar left to put in their silver cigar-cases."

"That driver is sure of heaven, anyhow," said the Sphinx.

"Perhaps, dear, when the time comes for us to arrive there, we will find him driving the station bus—who knows? But it was a pretty story, I must say. That driver deserves to be decorated."

"That's what I thought," said the Sphinx, eagerly.

"Yes! We might start a new society: The League of Kind Hearts; a Society for the Encouragement of Acts of Kindness. How would that do? Or we might endow a fund to bear the name of your 'bus-driver, and to be devoted in perpetuity to supplying destitute smokers with choice cigars."

"Yes," said the Sphinx, musingly, "that driver made me thoroughly ashamed of myself. I wish I was as sure of heaven as he is."

"But you are heaven," I whispered; "and à propos of heaven, here is a little song which I wrote for you last night, and with which I propose presently to settle the bill. I call it the Silver Girl:

   Whiter than whiteness was her breast,
And softer than new fallen snow,
So pure a peace, so deep a rest,

Yet purer peace below.

    Her face was like a moon-white flower
That swayed upon an ivory stem,
Her hair a whispering silver shower,
    Each foot a silver gem.

    And in a fair white house of dreams,
With hallowed windows all of pearl,
She sat amid the haunted gleams,
    That little silver girl;

    Sat singing songs of snowy white,
And watched all day, with soft blue eyes,
Her white doves flying in her sight,
    And fed her butterflies.

    Then when the long white day was passed,
The white world sleeping in the moon,
White bed, and long white sleep at last—
    She will not waken soon.

II—Words Written to Music

It is one of the many advantages of that simplicity of taste which is ignorance, that an incorrigible capacity for connoisseurship in the sister arts of cookery and music should enable one to be as happy with a bad dinner eaten to the sound of bad music, as others whose palates are attuned to the Neronian nightingales, and whose ears admit no harmonies less refined than the be-jewelled harmonies of Chopin.

I have eaten dinners delicate as silverpoints, in rooms of canary-coloured quiet, where the candles burn hushedly in their little silken tents, and the soft voices of lovers rise and fall upon the dreaming ear; but I confess that it was the soothing quiet, the healing tones of light and colour, and the face of the Sphinx irradiated by some dream of halcyon's tongues à la Persane, rather than the beautiful food, that inspired my passionate peace. Mere roast lamb, new potatoes and peas of living green had made me just as happy, gastronomically speaking, and I dare not mention what I order sometimes, and even day after day with a love that never tires, when I dine alone. Alone!

. . . the very word is like a bell
To toll me back from thee to my sole self;

for even this very night have I dined alone in a great solitude of social faces, low necks, electric lights, and the spirited band that has given me more pleasure than any music in London, always excepting my Bayreuth, the barrel-organ. Yes! strange as it may seem, I had come deliberately to hear this music, and secondarily to eat this dinner. What effect selections from Sullivan and "The Shop Girl," in collaboration with the three-and-sixpenny table d'hôte, would have upon more educated digestions its concerns me not to inquire; on mine they produce a sort of agonised ecstasy of loneliness—and to-night as I sat at our little lonely table in a corner of the great gallery and looked out across the glittering peristyle, ate that dinner and listened to that music, I shuddered with joy at my fearful loneliness.

I might have dined with the Beautiful, or have sent a telegraphic invitation to the Witty, I might have sat at meat with the Wise; but no! I would dine instead with the memories or dinners that were gone, and as the music did Miltonic battle near the ceiling, marched with clashing tread, or danced on myriad silken feet, wailed like the winds of the world, or laughed like the sun, my solitude grew peopled awhile with shapes fair and kind, who sat with me and lifted the glass and gave me their deep eyes, ladies who had intelligence in love, as Dante wrote, ladies of great gentleness and consolation, for whom God be thanked. But always in my ears, whatever the piece that was a-playing, the music came sweeping with dark surge across my fantasy, as though a sudden wind had dashed open a warm window, and let in a black night of homeless seas.

For in truth one I loved was out to-night on dark seas. She fares out across an ocean I have never sailed, to a land of which no man knows; and for her voyage she has only her silver feet, walking the inky waters, and the great light of her holy face to guide her steps. Ah! that I were with her tonight, walking hand in hand those dark waters. Oh, wherefore slip away thus companionless, fearless little voyager? Was it that I was unworthy to voyage those seas with you, that the weight of my mortality would have dragged down your bright immortality—youngest of the immortals. . . . But from that sea which the Divine alone may tread, comes back no answer, nor light of any star; but there has stolen to my side and kissed my brow, a shape dearer than all the rest, dear beyond dearness, a little earthly-heavenly shape who always comes when the rest have gone, and loves to find me sitting alone. She it is who leans her cheek against mine as I try to read beautiful words out of the dead man's book at my side, she it is who whispers that we shall be too late to find a seat in the pit unless we hurry, and she it is who gaily takes my arm as we trot off together on happy feet. The great commissionaire takes no note of her, he thinks I am alone; besides we seldom go in hansoms, and seldom sit in stalls. . . . Enough, O, music! be merciful. Be lonely no more, lest you break the heart of the lonely.

"Ah! you have never seen her!" I whisper to myself as the waiter brings me my coffee—and I look at him again with a certain curiosity as I think that he has never seen her. Never to have seen her!

And then presently, as if in pity, the music will change, perhaps it will play some sustaining song of faith, and strike a sort of glory across one's heart, the haughty heart of sorrow; or it will be human and gay, and suddenly turn this solitude of diners into a sort of family gathering of humanity, throwing open sad hearts that, like oneself, appear to be doing nothing but dine, and giving one glimpses into dreaming heads, linking all in one great friendship of common joys and sorrows, the one sweet beginning, and the one mysterious end.

In this mood faces one has seen more than once become friends, and I confess that the sight of certain waiters moving in their accustomed places almost moved me to tears. Such is the pathos of familiarity.

So my thoughts took another turn, and I fell to thinking with tenderness of the friends about town that the Sphinx and I had made in our dinings—friends whom it had cost us but a few odd shillings and sixpences to make, yet friends we had fancied we might trust, and even seek in a day of need. If they found me starving some night in the streets, I think they would take me in; and I think I know a coffee-stall man who would give me an early-morning cup of coffee, and add a piece of cake, were I to come to him bare-footed some wintry dawn.

I have heard purists object to the smiles that are bought, as if smiles can or should be had for nothing, and as if it shows a bad nature in a waiter to smile more sweetly upon a shilling than a penny. After all, is he so far wrong in deeming the heart that prompts the shilling better worth a smile than the reluctant hand of copper? Besides, we are never so mean to ourselves as when we are mean to others. A few shillings per annum sown about town will surround the path of the diner with smiles year in and year out. The doors fly open as by magic at his approach, and the cosiest tables in a dozen restaurants are in perpetual reserve for him. I am even persuaded that a consistent generosity to cabmen gets known in due course among the fraternity, and that thus, in process of time, the nicest people may rely on getting the nicest hansoms—though this may be a dream. Certain I am that it brings luck to be kind to a pathetic race of men for whom I have a special tenderness, those amateur footmen, the cab-openers. Have you ever noticed the fine manners of some or them, and their lover-like gentleness with the silk skirts that it is theirs to save from soilure of muddy wheels? A practical head might reflect how much they do towards keeping down your wife's dressmaker's bills. I daresay they save her a dress a year—and yet they are not treated with gratitude as a race. How involuntarily one seems to assume that they will accept nothing over a penny, and how fingers, not penurious on other occasions, automatically reject silver as they ferret in pence-pockets for suitable alms. No! not alms—payment, and sometimes poor payment, for a courtesy that adds another smile to your illusion or a smiling world.

Among the many lessons I have learnt from the Sphinx is one of the fair wage of the cab-opener. It was the very afternoon she had seen that cigar fall down from heaven, and her mood was thus the more attuned to pity. As we were about to drive away from the place of our lunching, having been ushered to our hansom by a tatterdemalion of distinguished manners, but marred unhappy countenance, I fumbled so long for the regulation twopence, that it seemed likely he should miss his reward or be run over in running after it. But at that moment the Sphinx's hand shot past mine and dropped something into the outstretched palm. The man took it mechanically, and in a second his face flashed surprise. Evidently she had given him something extravagant. She was watching for his look, and telegraphed a smile that she meant it. Then you never saw such a figure of grateful joy as that shabby fellow became. His face fairly shone, and for a few moments he ran by our cabside wildly waving his hat, with an indescribable emotion of affectionate thankfulness.

"What did you give him dear?" I asked.

"Never mind!"

"It wasn't a sovereign?"

"Never mind."

So I have never known what coin it was that thus transfigured him, but of this I am sure: that when the time of the great Terror has come to London, when the red flags wave on the barricades, and the puddles of red blood beneath the great guillotine in Trafalgar Square luridly catch the setting sun, the Sphinx and I will have a friend in that poor cab-opener.

There is another friend to whom we should fly for safety in those days of wrath. He, too, is a cab-opener, but, so to say, of higher rank—for he is the voluntary manager of a thriving cab-rank which we often have occasion to patronise. For some unknown reason he is always addressed as "Cap'n," and we never omit the courtesy as we salute him. So we have come to know him as The Captain of the Cab Rank. He is a short, thick-set, sturdy little man, with an overcoat buttoned straight beneath his chin, hands deep in his pockets, a firm, determined step, and a fiery face. He walks his pavement like a veritable captain on his quarter-deck, and his "Hansom up!" rings out like a stern word of command. At the call a shining door of the tavern opposite is thrown open with a slam, and a wild figure of a driver clatters across in terrified haste, and with his head still wrapped in the warm glow he has just forsaken, he climbs his dark throne, and once more shakes the weary reins. Then, as the little Captain briskly shut us in, with a salute that seems to say that he has thus given us a successful start in life, and it is not his fault if we don't go on as we've begun, he blows a shrill note upon his whistle, half to call up the next cab to its place in the rank, half to signalise our departure, as when sometimes a great boat sets out to sea they fire guns in the harbour, and excited crowds wave weeping handkerchiefs from the pier.

Yes! There are many faces I meet daily, faces I do business with and faces I take down to dinner, faces or the important and the brilliant, that I should miss much less than the little Captain of the Cab Rank. Our intercourse is of the slightest, we have little opportunities of studying each other's nature, and yet he is strangely vivid in my consciousness, quite a necessary figure in my picture of the world—so stamped is every part of him with that most appealing and attaching of all qualities, that of our common human nature. He has the great gift of character, and however poor and humble his lot, failure is surely no word to describe him, for he is a personality, and to be a personality is to have succeeded in life.

Yes! I often think of the Captain as I think of the famous characters in fiction, or notable figures in history; and I should feel very proud if I could believe he sometimes thought of me.

Well, well. . . . it is late. The bill, waiter, please! Good night! Good-night!

Two Prose Fancies

I—Sleeping Beauty

"Every woman is a sleeping beauty," I said, sententiously. "Only some need more waking than others?" replied my cynical friend.

"Yes, some will only awaken at the kiss of great love or great genius, which are not far from the same thing," I replied.

"I see," said the gay editor with whom I was talking.

Our conversation was of certain authors of our acquaintance, and how they managed their inspiration, of what manner were their muses, and what the methods of their stimulus. Some, we had noted, throve on constancy, to others inconstancy was the lawless law of their being; and so accepted had become these indispensable conditions of their literary activity that the wives had long since ceased to be jealous of the other wives. To a household dependent on poetry, constancy in many cases would mean poverty, and certain good literary wives had been known to rate their husbands with a lazy and unproductive faithfulness. The editor sketched a tragic mènage known to him, where the husband, a lyric poet of fame, had become so chronically devoted to his despairing wife that destitution stared them in the face. It was in vain that she implored him, with tears in her eyes, to fall in love with some other woman. She, she alone, he said, must be his inspiration; but as the domesticated muse is too often a muse of exquisite silence, too happy to sing its happiness, this lawful passion, which might otherwise have been turned to account, was unproductive too.

"And such a pretty woman," said the editor sympathetically. Of another happier case of domestic hallucination, he made the remark: "Says he owes it all to his wife! and you never saw such a plain woman in your life."

"How do you know she is plain?" I asked; "mayn't it be that the husband's sense of beauty is finer than yours? Do you think all beauty is for all men? or that the beauty all can see is best worth seeing?"

And then we spoke the words of wisdom and wit which I have written in ebony on the lintel of this little house of words. He who would write to live must talk to write, and I confess that I took up this point with my friend, and continued to stick to it, no doubt to his surprise, because I had at the moment some star-dust on the subject nebulously streaming and circling through my mind, which I was anxious to shape into something of an ordered world. So I talked not to hear myself speak, but to hear myself think, always, I will anticipate the malicious reader in saying, an operation of my mind of delightful unexpectedness.

"Why! you're actually thinking," chuckles one's brain to itself, "go on. Dance while the music's playing," and so the tongue goes dancing with pretty partners of words, till suddenly one's brain gives a sigh, the wheels begin to slow down, and music and dancing stop together, till some chance influence, a sound, a face, a flower, how or whence we know not, comes to wind it up again.

The more one ponders the mystery of beauty, the more one realises that the profoundest word in the philosophy of aesthetics is that of the simple-subtle old proverb: Beauty is in the eyes of the beholder. Beauty, in fact, is a collaboration between the beholder and the beheld. It has no abstract existence, and is visible or invisible as one has eyes to see or not to see it, that is, as one is endowed or not endowed with the sense of beauty, an hieratic sense which, strangely enough, is assumed as common to humanity. Particularly is this assumption made in regard to the beauty of women. Every man, however beauty-blind he may really be, considers himself a judge of women—though he might hesitate to call himself a judge of horses. Far indeed from its being true that the sense of beauty is universal, there can be little doubt that the democracy is for the most part beauty-blind, and that while it has a certain indifferent pleasure in the comeliness that comes of health, and the prettiness that goes with ribbons, it dislikes and fears that finer beauty which is seldom comely, never pretty, and always strange.

National galleries of art are nothing against this truth. Once in a while the nation may rejoice over the purchase of a bad picture it can understand, but for the most part—what to it are all these strange pictures, with their disquieting colours and haunted faces? What recks the nation at large of its Bellinis or its Botticellis? what even of its Titians or its Tintorettos? Was it not the few who bought them, with the money of the many, for the delight of the few?

Well, as no one would dream of art-criticism by plébiscite, why should universal conventions of the beauty of women find so large an acceptance merely because they are universal? There are vast multitudes, no doubt, who deem the scented-soap beauties of Bouguereau more beautiful than the strange ladies of Botticelli, and, were you to inquire, you would discover that your housemaid wonders to herself, as she dusts your pictures to the sound of music-hall song, what you can see in the plain lean women of Burne-Jones, or the repulsive ugliness of "The Blessed Damosel." She thanks heaven that she was not born with such a face, as she takes a reassuring glance in the mirror at her own regular prettiness, and more marketable bloom. For, you see, this beauty is still asleep for her—as but a few years ago it was asleep for all but the artists who first kissed it awake.

All beauty was once asleep like that, even the very beauty your housemaid understands and perhaps exemplifies. It lay asleep awaiting the eye of the beholder, it lay asleep awaiting the kiss of genius; and, just as one day nothing at all seemed beautiful, so some day all things will come to seem so, if the revelation be not already complete.

For indeed much beauty that was asleep fifty years ago has been passionately awakened and given a sceptre and a kingdom since then: the beauty of lonely neglected faces that no man loved, or loved only by stealth, for fear of the mockery of the blind, the beauty of unconventional contours and unpopular colouring, the beauty of pallor, of the red-haired, and the fausse maigre. The fair and the fat are no longer paramount, and the beauty of forty has her day.

Nor have the discoveries of beauty been confined to the faces and forms of women. In Nature too the waste places where no man sketched or golfed have been reclaimed for the kingdom of beauty. The little hills had not really rejoiced us till Wordsworth came, but we had learnt his lesson so well that the beauty of the plain slept for us all the longer, till with Tennyson and Millet, it awakened at last—the beauty of desolate levels, solitary moorlands, and the rich melancholy of the fens.

Wherever we turn our eyes, we find the beauty of character supplanting the beauty of form, or if not supplanting, asserting its claim to a place beside the haughty sister who would fain keep Cinderella, red-headed and retroussée, in the background—yes! and for many even supplanting! It is only when regularity of form and personal idiosyncrasy and intensity of character are united in a face, that the so-called classical beauty is secure of holding its own with those whose fealty most matters—and that union to any triumphant degree is exceedingly rare. Even when that union has come about there are those, in this war of the classicism and romanticism of faces, who would still choose the face dependent on pure effect for its charm; no mask of unchanging beauty, but a beauty whose very life is change, and whose magic, so to say, is a miraculous accident, elusive and unaccountable.

Miraculous and unaccountable! In a sense all beauty is that, but in the case of the regular, so to say, authorised beauty, it seems considerably less so. For in such faces, the old beauty-masters will tell you, the brow is of such a breadth and shape, the nose so long, the mouth shaped in this way, and the eyes set and coloured in that; and thus, of this happy marriage of proportions, beauty has been born. This they will say in spite of the everyday fact of thousands of faces being thus proportioned and coloured without the miracle taking place, ivory lamps in which no light of beauty burns. And it is this fact that proves the truth of the newer beauty we are considering. Form is thus seen to be dependent on expression, though expression, the new beauty-masters would contend, is independent of form. For the new beauty there are no such rules; it is, so to say, a prose beauty, for which there is no formulated prosody, entirely free and individual in its rhythms, and personal in its effects. Sculpture is no longer its chosen voice among the arts, but rather music with its myriad meanings, and its infinitely responsive inflections.

You will hear it said of such beauty—that it is striking, individual, charming, fascinating and so on, but not exactly beautiful. This, if you are an initiate of the new beauty, you will resist, and permit no other description but beauty—the only word which accurately expresses the effect made upon you. That such effect is not produced upon others need not depress you; for similarly you might say of the beauty that others applaud that for you it seems attractive, handsome, pretty, dainty and so on, but not exactly beautiful; or admitting its beauty, that it is but one of many types of beauty, the majority of which are neither straight-lined nor regular.

For when it is said that certain faces are not exactly beautiful, what is meant is that they fail to conform to one or other of the straight-lined types; but by what authority has it been settled once and for all that beauty cannot exist outside the straight line and the chubby curve? It matters not what authority one were to bring, for vision is the only authority in this matter, and the more ancient the authority the less is it final, for it has thus been unable to take account of all the types that have come into existence since its day, types spiritual, intellectual and artistic, born of the complex experience of the modern world.

And yet it has not been the modern world alone that has awakened that beauty independent of, and perhaps greater than, the beauty of form and colour; rather it may be said to have reawakened it by study of certain subtle old masters of the Renaissance; and the great beauties who have made the tragedies and love-stories of the world, so far as their faces have been preserved to us, were seldom "beautiful," as the populace would understand beauty. For perhaps the highest beauty is visible only to genius, or that great love which, we have said, is a form of genius. It was only, it will be remembered, at the kiss of a prince that Sleeping Beauty might open her wonderful eyes.

II—A Literary Omnibus

There were ten of us travelling life's journey together from Oxford Circus to the Bank, one to fall away early at Tottenham Court Road, leaving his place unfilled till we steamed into Holborn at Mudie's, where, looking up to make room for a new arrival, I perceived, with an unaccustomed sense of being at home in the world, that no less than four of us were reading. It became immediately evident that in the new arrival our reading party had made an acquisition, for he carried three books in a strap, and to the fourth, a dainty blue cloth volume with rough edges, he presently applied a paper-knife with that eager tenderness which there is no mistaking. The man was no mere lending library reader. He was an aristocrat, a poet among readers, a bookman who sang. We were all more or less of the upper crust ourselves, with the exception of a dry and dingy old gentleman in the remote corner who, so far as I could determine, was deep in a digest of statutes. His interest in the new-comer was merely an automatic raising of the head as the bus stopped, and an automatic sinking of it back again as we once more rumbled on. The rest of us, however, were not so poorly satisfied. This fifth reader to our coach had suddenly made us conscious of our freemasonry, and henceforward there was no peace for us till we had, by the politest stratagems of observation, made out the titles of the books from which as from beakers our eyes were silently and strenuously drinking such different thoughts and dreams.

The lady third from the door on the side facing me was reading a book which gave me no little trouble to identify, for she kept it pressed on her lap with tantalising persistence, and the headlines, which I was able to spell out with eyes grown telescopic from curiosity, proved those tiresome headlines which refer to the contents of chapter or page instead of considerately repeating the title of the book. It was not a novel. I could tell that, for there wasn't a scrap of conversation, and it wasn't novelist's type. I watched like a lynx to catch a look at the binding. Suddenly she lifted it up, I cannot help thinking out of sheer kindness, and it proved to be a stately unfamiliar edition of a book I should have known well enough, simply The French Revolution. Why will people tease one by reading Carlyle in any other edition but the thin little octavos, with the sticky brown and black bindings of old?

The pretty dark-haired girl next but one on my own side, what was she reading? No! . . . But she was, really!

Need I say that my eyes beat a hasty retreat to my little neighbour, the new-comer, who sat facing me next to the door, one of whose books in the strap I had instantly recognised as Weir of Hermiston. Of the other two, one was provokingly turned with the edges only showing, and of the edges I couldn't be quite sure, though I was almost certain they belonged to an interesting new volume of poems I knew of. The third had the look of a German dictionary. But, of course, it was the book he was reading that was the chief attraction, and I rather like to think that probably I was the only one of his fellow travellers who succeeded in detecting the honey-pot from which he was delicately feeding. It took me some little time, though the book, with its ribbed blue cover gravely lined with gold and its crisp rose-yellow paper, struck me with instant familiarity. "Preface to Second Edition," deciphered backwards, was all I was able to make out at first, for the paper-knife loitered dreamily among the opening pages, till at last with the turning of a page, the prose suddenly gave place to a page prettily broken up with lines and half-lines of italics, followed by a verse or two—and "Of course," I exclaimed to myself, with a curious involuntary gratitude, "it is Dr. Wharton's Sappho."

And so it was. That penny bus was thus carelessly carrying along the most priceless of written words. We were journeying in the same conveyance with

"Like the sweet apple which reddens upon the topmost bough,
A-top on the topmost twig—which the pluckers forgot somehow—
Forgot it net, nay, but got it not, for none could get it till now."

"I loved thee,
At this, long ago."

with

"The moon has set, and the Pleiades; it is midnight, the time is going by, and I sleep alone."

 Yes, it was no less a presence than Sappho's that had stepped in amongst us at the corner of New Oxford Street. Visibly it had been a little black-bearded bookman, rather French in appearance, possibly a hard-worked teacher of languages—but actually it had been Sappho. So strange are the contrasts of the modern world, so strange the fate of beautiful words. Two thousand five hundred years! So far away from us was the voice that had suddenly called to us, a lovely apparition of sound, as we trundled dustily from Oxford Circus to the Bank.

"The moon has set, and the Pleiades; it is midnight, the time is going by, and I sleep alone," I murmured, as the conductor dropped me at Chancery Lane.